Security Breach of the Heart

A Romantic Suspense Story

Miranda Herald

My Koala Pouch

Contents

Also By Miranda Herald

Loves Cats Series:

Prequel Chapters: Willa's Blooper Reel- FREE at https://dl.bookfunnel.com/yqs4i2iqr0

Book 1: Loves Cats, Anonymous

Book 2: Swipe Right for More Cats

Puzzling through Romance Series:

Prequel Novella: Blundering through Paradise- FREE at

https://dl.bookfunnel.com/q22azd8n2k

Book 1: Outwitting Paradise

Book 2: Misplacing Paradise

Book 3: Hiding Paradise

Book 4: Delivering Paradise

Smitten Scientists:

Catch and Release

Love, Lies and Investigations:

Security Breach of the Heart

<u>Briarhaven Chronicles</u>

Practical Guide Series:

Practical Guide to Magical Farming

Direwolf Series:

A Wolf in Sheep's Clothing

Chapter One: The Case of Bypassing Security

A *drianna*

Adrianna looked up at the giant cave mouth looming in front of her. She shifted her weight from one foot to the other, nervous about her first day at work. She made her feet move closer to the highly secure mountain that was so large it felt like it was about to swallow her whole.

In front of her stood a fence that was gated shut and at least sixteen feet high, with barbed wire along the upper edge. A man stood on a small platform on the top of the guardroom, watching everyone approaching, with an automatic rifle swung across his back. She watched as a large, plain white van pulled up and was thoroughly searched before entering the fence.

She took a deep breath and looked down at herself, smoothing her brand-new black blazer and straightening the matching skirt. Her blonde hair hung in waves around her heart-shaped face. She'd been waiting for months for her security clearances to go through, and now was the big day.

Squaring her shoulders, she entered the small guard room and waited in line. There were two guards checking everyone in. She watched the employees in front of her routinely scan their badges and type a code into a number pad. A small green light went off on a locked half door that allowed the person to enter the other side of the guardroom, where they placed their bags and lunches in an X-ray machine and walked through a metal detector.

When it was her turn, she walked up to the closest security guard, or at least got as near as the half wall would allow. The security guard was sitting in front of a screen showing the X-rayed bags. She cleared her throat and fiddled with her thumbs while she waited for him to look up and acknowledge her.

He stood up and walked around the X-ray machine, but stayed on his side of the half wall. Initially, the sight of a long, jagged scar running down his face startled her. It started slightly above his eye, slicing through his eyebrow, ran down his cheek, and ended at his chin. After her initial shock, she noticed he was otherwise a good-looking man, with short brown hair and a trim security guard uniform.

She spoke first. "Hello. B.I.S.S. recently hired me. They took my picture at their above-ground office location and told me that my badge would be waiting here for me today."

The man gave her a charming smile that drew her focus away from the distracting scar. His other cheek sported a deep dimple. "Welcome to the Limestone Vault. I'll get you settled. What's your name, date of birth, and social security number?" It may have been a lot of information for a stranger to ask her, but after months of investigators questioning her friends and relatives about every aspect of her life, she was getting used to it.

"My name is Adrianna Ettans, my birthday is on June 4th, 1992, and my social security number is 186-77-9090." Smiling, she looked at him and added a bit more in total exasperation over all of their security measures. "... and my height is five-foot, five inches, and my favorite color is periwinkle."

Chuckling, the man said, "I'm sure you had to go through a lot of rigmarole to get in here. Let me get your badge." She glanced at the badge hanging on a lanyard around his neck. It read: Greg Anderson.

He called out to the other security guard, "Hey, Jim, I'm getting a new employee set up. I need you to process the inbounds." Then he walked over to a computer, typed some things in, made a phone call, and then opened up a drawer and dug around for a few moments.

He sauntered back over and held out his hand with her badge hanging from a lanyard. "Here you go. That will get you inside every day. Your pin code is 4052. Memorize that or your badge will get locked out, and it's a big to-do to get it working again. Don't forget your badge because you will need to scan it every day when you enter or leave the Limestone Vault facility. Do you have any questions?"

Biting her lip, she asked, "Um, what do I do now?"

Greg pointed his hand toward the half door. "Well, it's your turn to go through security. Scan your badge, and then you have thirty seconds to input your code. Place everything you brought with you on the X-ray's conveyor belt. If you have anything metal on you, like a key chain, belt, or steel-toed shoes, place them in the bin and push it on the conveyor belt too. I didn't see any alerts about any orthopedic implants when I got you set up in the system, so you shouldn't have to worry about that."

Her eyes were wide, and her eyebrows furrowed as she chewed on her lip again. "Thank you so much. Would you mind giving me some directions to find my way to the B.I.S.S. headquarters inside? Are there signs?"

"Actually, I called your office while I was getting your badge situated. There should be someone here to escort you shortly. It's an unlabeled maze down there, and you don't want to go wandering around on your own."

With those last *reassuring* words, Greg went back to his post, looking through the X-rayed bags. A droplet of sweat trickled down her forehead as she made her way through security. She gave a breath of relief when she arrived at the end and picked up her bag, but Greg gently tapped her arm to catch her attention and stop her. "Ma'am, please step over here for a moment."

Adrianna's eyes grew large, and her heart thudded as she took a few steps out of the entry path. "What's the matter? Did I do something wrong?"

He pointed to her bags. "I need to request that you leave your cellphone here. We do not allow any cameras or recording devices in the Vault. Next time, I would suggest leaving it in your car or at home, but for today, I will bag it and you can collect it here on your way out. Don't worry, I'll take good care of it."

Digging around in her purse, she pulled out her phone. For a second, she thought he was trying to get her phone number in the oddest way possible, but it made sense. They wouldn't go through all this trouble to make this space so secure, only to allow people to take pictures of the secure information willy-nilly.

Unfortunately, their security protocols didn't protect the information from someone's memory. She figured that must be why they were so thorough in the investigation process. She didn't have a photographic memory or anything, but she was great at remembering numbers and small bits of information. It was what made her so good at puzzles, and she hoped it would help her in becoming a good background investigator.

Greg gave her another smile. When she saw his dimple, she couldn't help but smile back. What a nice man with such a friendly personality. She wasn't very good at making friends, so she would be happy if her new coworkers were even half as friendly as him. Distracted by his scar once again, she tried to avert her eyes. *I wonder what happened to him.*

They both turned when they heard an older woman with short brown hair and glasses calling from beyond the half wall. "Hello! I need to talk to whoever is in charge here."

Taking Adrianna's phone from her, Greg gave her a wink. "I hope you have a great first day." Then he turned to the woman and called out, "One moment, ma'am, I'll be right with you." He placed Adrianna's phone in a bag, labeled it, placed it in a drawer, and then went over to talk to the woman.

Roughly five minutes later, Adrianna was shifting on her feet, wondering how long she should stand there waiting. She knew there were a few different companies that shared this highly secure subterranean facility, so it probably wasn't a good idea to just wander around. She looked through the other end of the security room and peeked into the large, dim cave mouth in front of her. *I guess I have no choice but to stay put for now.*

The loud woman from a few moments ago came to stand next to Adrianna, a new badge swinging around her neck. "These people certainly aren't making a good first impression on me by making me wait up here. I'm here on time, even if they aren't."

She turned to Adrianna. "My name is Judy. Today is my first day at Background Investigations and Security Services. The security guard told me to come and stand by you while I wait. What do you do here?"

Adrianna nodded her head. "Today is my first day at B.I.S.S, too. I've been waiting almost three months for my security clearances to come through, and the anticipation for today has been killing me!"

Judy made a harrumph sound. "Oh, I didn't think you looked like the type. Well, good luck to you. I hope you don't wash out."

Today is going to be a really long day.

Chapter Two: The Case in the Old Limestone Mine

Adrianna

None too soon, a tall skinny woman with dark skin, curly black hair, and a bright smile came to greet them. She had a cute little baby bump, and Adrianna guessed she was somewhere around five months pregnant.

"Hello! You must be Adrianna and Judy. My name is Henrietta from BISS, and I am going to be showing you around and training you two over the next few weeks. Are you ready?" Whereas Adrianna had carefully pronounced each letter of B.I.S.S., Henrietta turned the acronym into its own word, BISS.

Nodding her head, Adrianna was feeling much better after Henrietta's warm greeting. Judy gave Henrietta the first smile Adrianna had seen from her all morning. "I was just telling Adrianna here how I have waited almost three months for my background investigation to be complete and the anticipation of getting to work has been killing me!"

Adrianna frowned. "Yep, I'm ready to go." *If I say something about her repeating my words, I'm just going to sound petty. Why does she have it out for me?*

They left the small guard room and entered the large cave opening that was at least a hundred feet wide and fifty feet tall. Upon entering, her eyes took a moment to adjust to the dimness, then she stopped and gaped, no longer following closely behind Henrietta.

All the bare rock walls were whitewashed, and they'd cemented the floor. The interior was dimly lit by a strip of lights running along the ceiling of the cave, where exposed pipes, vents, and wires ran in all directions.

There were a few plain gray doors. She could see the stone block that surrounded the doors until they met the raw cave wall. The intersection of the block and the cave wall seemed to be covered in cement. All the doors she could see looked the same, except for the first one closest to the cave mouth. It had a large sign labeled *The Limestone Vault: A secure facility dedicated to protecting what's important.*

With Henrietta leading them down a main path of the cave, they passed several offshoots, all containing doors. She couldn't imagine what all was down here. Henrietta didn't seem to care about her surroundings at all, but Adrianna didn't know if she would ever get used to it.

Henrietta paused slightly to allow Adrianna to get her bearings and catch up, then she spoke almost constantly as Adrianna and Judy followed her. "As you may already know, BISS is short for Background Investigations and Security Services, but sometimes I refer to it as BS when I'm having a rough day."

They all chuckled as she continued. "BISS is in room 4B. They haven't labeled the tunnels and doors, so that isn't helpful unless you know the code. We are in the fourth tunnel from the entrance and the second door on the left. It takes about ten minutes to get from the parking lot through security and another ten minutes to walk from the mouth of the vault to our room, so I would suggest coming twenty to thirty minutes early each day, unless you speed walk."

Finally, Henrietta took a break, and Adrianna could ask a question. "Why aren't there any labels or signs on the doors?"

Pointing to one door they passed, she said, "We have never had someone break into the facility, but the lack of directions is a security precaution, just in case. It's a lot harder to find a specific room and steal something if you don't know what's inside each room."

They passed the third tunnel, and Henrietta pointed. A few people were talking in the walkway, watching them as they passed. "For example, it's rumored the third room in this branch of the cave is the vault for a famous cartoon movie creator. One of the other rooms is supposedly owned by a billionaire to store precious stones and gems. Our room is full of paper and people's identities."

A short passenger bus drove by on a skinny road that snaked through the Vault, carrying a lot of people. Adrianna realized the deeper they got into the cave, the dirtier the air felt. *I wonder how good the air circulation is in here, with vehicles driving around in such an enclosed area?*

Judy sounded slightly irked as she asked, "Why didn't we take the bus?"

Henrietta waved her hand at the bus dismissively. "You are welcome to use the bus if you want to. There is a bus stop in the parking lot across the street from the vault, and a few bus stops throughout the tunnels. Some people use it every day, but I find it a pain. The bus makes its round about every half-hour, but it's always running late, so you can't plan on it to pick you up specifically on the hour or the half-hour."

Pausing for a moment in the middle of the path, Henrietta leaned down and rubbed her calf for a moment and then continued walking. "What you end up doing is waiting in the parking lot for the bus to pick you up. It could be a few minutes or another half-hour. Then it stops at the gate where everyone has to get off and go through security, and then it picks everyone back up on the inside of the gate and makes multiple stops throughout the tunnels. It's a lot less frustrating and usually faster to just walk if you can."

They turned down the fourth tunnel from the cave entrance and walked to the second door. "Here, you each have to scan your badges before entering and leaving this room. You may not hold the door open for anyone who hasn't scanned their badge, because security needs a clear record of who is in each room in case of an emergency."

All three of them scanned their badges and entered the room. The door opened up into a football field-sized cave. All walls were white-washed, with hundreds of pipes, wires, and tubes crisscrossing near the vaulted cave ceiling. They carpeted the floor and built offices out of cinder block meshing against the original rock wall with cement. The middle of the room was covered with over a hundred cubicles, and Adrianna could see, in the back of the room, long metal shelving jam-packed with folders overflowing with papers.

Henrietta started walking into the room. "Follow me. I'll get you guys set up in your cubicles with your computers, and then we will begin training. We will spend most of the morning talking about the company, ethics, and keeping personal information secure, but by this afternoon I hope to have you processing your first type of background material. Birth certificates!"

Adrianna sat in the plain gray cubicle that was to be her home for this next part of her life. There was a computer with dual monitors and a desk drawer with standard office supplies. She would put up a few decorations and it would be her own private cozy spot. She put her purse in the drawer and shut it, feeling better that it now held something. *Will I be staring at these walls for the next few years?*

Shivering, Adrianna realized her cubicle seemed to be colder than most of the room. Looking up, she noticed she was sitting directly under an air vent. It was the middle of summer, and it may have been close to ninety degrees outside, but tomorrow she would bring an extra sweater to work.

After Henrietta helped them to get everything set up, she called Judy and Adrianna over. "Come on, let's give you a tour of the room, and I'll show you where we pick up materials to process." They walked over to the shelving containing thousands of files. A few people were rushing around, filing more folders as quickly as they could. "This is where we keep all active investigations."

Pointing to a series of shelving off to the side, Henrietta flipped through the papers until she took out a small stack of birth certificates. She handed them each a copy of a birth certificate. "This is the first type of material you are going to learn to process. We will take them with us to the training room, even though we won't be diving into them yet." Adrianna looked at her packet. Scanning the paper briefly with her eyes, she grew wide eyed. In the place-of-birth line it said an elevator in Brinton, Tennessee.

A tall, graying man in a gray suit sauntered down the row toward them. "Henrietta! Is this our new employees? Sorry I wasn't able to meet you two at your last interviews. There is so much to do down here that I don't get a lot of time above ground. My name is Darren, and I will be your team leader, so if you have any questions or concerns that your trainer can't help you with, feel free to come and see me. How has your first day at work been going so far?"

Sweet as can be, Judy smiled widely and answered first. "Today has been the most amazing experience. I am truly honored to be working here and will work my hardest for you, sir."

Smiling, he tapped the birth certificate in her hand. "I love to hear that enthusiasm! That's just the type of employees we want here. Positive go-getters that are already processing materials moments after walking in the door. I hope to see more of you in the coming months once you get up and running." He nodded his head and walked off.

Judy beamed at him until he turned away and then gave Adrianna a smirk. She was going to say a simple, "My day has been going great, Henrietta has been so helpful," but she never got the chance. She may not have been the best at idle chitchat, so her hard work would have to do the talking for her.

Henrietta shifted around and groaned. "We will get started on our training in a few minutes. If you two want to gather a pen and some paper from your desks, I have to run to the bathroom yet again, and I'll meet you over there in a few minutes."

Henrietta hurried off as Adrianna walked back to her cubicle. A blank cut-out paper handprint sat on her desk.

Chapter Three: The Case of the Missing Office

A *drianna*

Picking up the handprint, and turning it around in confusion, Adrianna noted it was adult-sized, but on the smaller size. There was a slight bump on the base of one finger where a ring might have been located, but otherwise, it was completely blank.

Henrietta came up behind her and started chuckling. "Looks like you need a hand. That's a harmless game that people who work here do to new employees. The idea is like a puzzle. They want to see what kind of investigator you would make some day. You can either find whose hand that belongs to, or you can just ignore it because it really doesn't matter."

Out of the corner of her eye, Adrianna saw Judy pick up a similar hand, crumple it up, and throw it in her garbage can. Setting it aside on her desk, Adrianna thought she would think about it for a bit. She loved puzzles.

Henrietta waved Judy over to Adrianna's desk. After she joined them, Henrietta pointed to the birth certificates still in her hands. "A background investigator is the person who goes out to someone's house and interviews them and follows up on any discrepancies. As background processors, we won't be out in the field. Our job is to find everything that is bad or questionable in every piece of material we process and document it. The final reviewer will look through all potential issues and determine whether to award a clearance after a person's entire file is processed piece by piece. I don't know the exact requirements for each level of clearance, but all we have to worry about in this job is not letting any potential issues slip through."

She pointed at the name on the birth certificate she held. "What we are looking for in this document is any discrepant or missing information. Anything that could be used for leverage against someone in the future. Basically, if you see anything that looks out of place, write it down, no matter how small it may seem to you. For example, if a father is missing on a birth certificate, we will notate it for the reviewer. Most likely, it won't make a difference in the end, but you never know; we may find a reason he isn't listed on the document. We will check the birth date with what we have in our computer system and make sure that they are a United States citizen."

Henrietta's stomach audibly grumbled, and she put her hand on her baby bump. "Alright, it's been a long morning already. Why don't you guys have lunch, and we will pick up with this again afterwards? You are welcome to leave this room or the vault as you please. Just use your badge to sign in and out. I'll see you back here in half an hour."

Adrianna sat at her desk and munched on her sandwich. She tapped her fingers while looking over the handprint. So far, she was pretty sure it belonged to a married woman, but that could still be over fifty different people in this room. Judy got up and left, and Adrianna stealthily grabbed the handprint out of her otherwise empty garbage can. She unwrinkled it. Bingo! It belonged to the same person as her hand, but on Judy's hand, she caught sight of a bit of blue ink on the side of the hand where someone traced it with a permanent marker.

Looking at the clock on her computer, Adrianna saw she still had twenty minutes left in her lunch break and had no clue what to do with her time. A thought struck her. It took about ten minutes to get out to the mouth of the cave and ten minutes to get back. A little sunlight and leg stretching would feel good.

Now that she had a mission, she moved swiftly back to the tunnels, scanning her badge as she left. Speed walking down the cave's tunnels, Adrianna stopped in the sunlight but didn't go through the nearby guardhouse. She didn't want to bother with going back through security. She soaked in the warm sunlight and tipped her head upwards, thankful for the rays beating down on her after being in the cold, dim cave all morning.

She heard a shout from the rooftop of the guard's house, and Adrianna opened her eyes. She squinted past the bright sunshine. Greg stood up there with an amused smile on his face. "Sunbathing, are you? Your name's Adrianna, right? My name's Greg."

Lifting her hand to shield her eyes from the sunlight, she smiled. "Nice to formally meet you, Greg, even if I have to do it shouting. Yes, my name is Adrianna, and I came out here to soak up a few rays of sunshine. I would love to stand out here on this beautiful day longer, but I actually need to get back. My lunch break is almost over."

Nodding his head, Greg shouted, "Have a good rest of your first day!"

Shouting back, "Thanks!" Adrianna turned and speed walked back down the tunnels. Smiling to herself, she couldn't help thinking about what a nice guy Greg was. It would be nice to be greeted by such a cheery person each day. Reaching for her pocket to check how much time she had left, Adrianna realized she didn't have her phone on her anymore. *Looks like I'm going to need to invest in a watch.*

The maze of tunnels and doors looked similar to her. She was daydreaming for a little bit, but she was pretty sure this was the fourth tunnel from the entrance. She went to the first door and scanned her badge, but a red light came on. *Oh no. I'm at the wrong door. How in the world will I find the right one?*

Her heart pounded as her anxiety made her body go into fight-or-flight mode. Knowing she would be late, Adrianna didn't see any other option but to backtrack and count the tunnels more carefully as she made her way to the BISS headquarters. She walked as fast as she could back to the entrance.

She ran scenarios through her head about how she would explain being late on her first day on the job. Should she tell the truth, that she got lost, or make something up that would make her look more responsible? Maybe security stopped her and delayed her or maybe she had to help someone who fell and got hurt. While she loved solving puzzles, she didn't have the best poker face, so she decided to stick with the truth and suffer the consequences.

After reaching the cave mouth again, Adrianna tried to stay as professional as she could, as she half ran and half jogged back to her room. She passed a few people who looked at her oddly as she rushed by, but none of them were dressed as professionally as the people she saw in BISS's room, so she didn't think they would head to the same place.

After carefully counting the fourth tunnel and going to the first door, her badge still flashed red. She gave a frustrated groan as a man opened the door she was standing in front of. She saw around him that the room behind this door was small and contained only a few shelves and boxes. It was definitely the wrong room. He looked at her suspiciously. "Who are you, and what are you doing trying to get to my jewels?"

Chapter Four:
The Case of the Smuggled Cat

*A*drianna

Adrianna stammered out an apology. "I'm sorry. I wasn't trying to get to anything. Today is my first day on the job, and I had the wrong door."

He frowned, and a slight growl escaped under his breath as he said, "BISS?"

She nodded her head with her eyes open wide.

Pointing to the next door over, the man sharply said, "You'd think the people they hired would have some brains after all the hoops they make you jump through to work there. Your door is over there. Make sure you don't get them mixed up again."

"Sorry, sir. It won't happen again," she quickly replied as she scurried down to the correct door. She scanned her badge, and it turned green this time. With a sigh of relief, she made her way back to her desk, where Judy and Henrietta were waiting.

Henrietta looked at her own watch. "You're about fifteen minutes late. It's not a big deal on your first day, but make sure you don't make a habit of it. Now, as I was saying..."

Motioning Adrianna and Judy to join her, Henrietta went to her own desk. "Actually, come with me. It's easier for me to show you how things work on my computer for the first time."

As quick as can be, Henrietta used her fingerprint to log onto her computer, then clicked on an icon with a B on it. Her screen immediately turned black, with green letters along the top in an old-fashioned font. "This is the computer system we use to process background investigations. It is DOS based, so it's not the most intuitive, but it is secure from most hacking and malware. I will teach you how to use it because this is the database where everyone's background information is stored and accessed.

"Just an FYI. Your employee number will automatically sign every piece of material when you put it into this database. Be careful that you don't make mistakes. These are people's livelihoods that depend on our work being accurate. You don't want to put a serious issue on someone's otherwise clean record accidentally or they could lose a job opportunity. Likewise, you don't want someone with a serious issue to be missed because they could be a security risk for the government or whatever company needs the background investigation completed.

"So, let's look at this first birth certificate on my pile. The names and birthdays match, and they were born in the United States. We have processed that one piece of information for this background investigation, so we will go in and put an NI next to the birth certificate because there were no issues. That's my employee number next to it because I was the one who processed it. This person will also need a credit report and a field investigator report to be processed before we send it to a reviewer."

They went through the rest of the pile of birth certificates and learned how to process them on their own computers. The computer system was going to take a lot of getting used to, but Adrianna wrote notes about where each of the "F keys" took her and what commands she needed to type in to get her where she needed to go. Her brain hurt, but she hoped she would catch on soon.

When her brain didn't feel like it could hold any new information, Henrietta handed her a new credit report. Henrietta, cheerful as ever, told her, "We are going to mark any issues you see here from A to D, depending on the severity of the problem. An A is something that isn't too bad, like a 30-day-past-due notice, but a D is something more serious, like a bankruptcy."

By the end of her day, Adrianna walked out of the tunnels feeling like her brain was mush. She didn't think she'd ever tried to cram so much information in there before. *Maybe I'm not cut out for this job after all.* She thought she was imagining things as she heard a soft "meow" near the front of the cave. Was her brain fried? Was she hearing things now?

A few people passed her on their way out for the day. None of them seemed to have heard anything, but her curiosity got the best of her. She was in no hurry to get back to the small cottage she was renting. It was cute, but also empty and in the middle of nowhere.

She couldn't help but take a peek. Roughly one hundred feet back from the mouth of the cave, she heard another soft meow. A young calico cat crouched deep in a crevice of the cave. The poor thing looked skinny and scared and was too far to reach.

Taking out the last of her sandwich she had never finished at lunchtime, she pulled out some lunch meat and set it on the ground near her feet. The cat didn't move, just eyed her warily. She tried setting out a bit of lunch meat closer to the crevice and stepped back. The calico cat crawled out of the crevice, stomach close to the floor and ears alert. It cautiously and delicately nibbled on the food, then finished the rest in one big gulp. She looked up at Adrianna and meowed.

Adrianna set out a trail of food so the cat eventually came right to her. The cat scratched at her new blazer as she tried to pick it up. She got the poor frightened creature to calm down, but not before tearing a hole in her blazer and making her hand bleed slightly. The cat had no collar or other form of identification.

With the cat held firmly against her chest, Adrianna slowly stood up and walked out to the guardhouse. She hoped nothing in there startled the cat. What in the world was she going to do with this cat? She was used to working long hours and sometimes even forgot to feed herself. She wasn't ready to care for a pet. In her last apartment, she couldn't even keep a plant alive.

Greg spotted her as she walked in the door. He raised his eyebrow as he seemed to take in the cat, her ruined blazer, and bleeding hand. "Well, it certainly looks like you have had an eventful first day on the job!" He frowned. "You know you're not allowed to bring your pet to work, right? I watched as we screened your bags. How in the world did you smuggle that little guy in?"

Chapter Five: The Case of the Employee Theft

G *reg* Greg passed through security and walked up to the massive opening of the Limestone Vault, the high-security underground facility where he worked as a security guard. The hole loomed in front of him, silent and imposing, but it was just another day at the office for him. Greg took a deep breath and stepped through a small man door, stepping into the cool, dimly lit interior of the facility.

He made his way down the long corridor, passing by the monitoring station where his colleague, Jeremy, was stationed for his own shift. Jeremy nodded to him, his eyes fixed on the screens in front of him, monitoring the various security feeds that crisscrossed the underground complex. Greg paused by his friend's chair. "Hey, Jeremy, keeping an eye on our cave today?"

Jeremy looked up from the screens and grinned. "You know it, man. The Limestone Vault is Fort Knox compared to the other places I've worked."

Greg chuckled. "Oh, I can imagine. So, anything exciting happening on the monitors today?"

Jeremy rolled his eyes playfully. "Oh yeah, the most thrilling thing ever—someone left their coffee cup in the break room."

Greg laughed. "Oh no, we've got a serious security breach on our hands!"

Jeremy joined in the laughter. "Yeah, I might have to call in the big guns for this one. It's a real crisis."

Greg shook his head, still chuckling. "Well, I'll keep an eye out for any rogue coffee cups during my rounds. We can't have them compromising our top-secret facility."

Jeremy smirked. "Thanks, Greg. I knew I could count on you. Now, I just need to find a way to not go out of my mind from boredom because of staring at these screens all day."

With a friendly wave, Greg continued on his rounds, leaving Jeremy to his monitoring duties. Their lighthearted banter had eased some of the tension Greg felt in the high-security environment, and he felt grateful for the camaraderie they shared. It made the challenging work they did at the Limestone Vault just a little easier to manage.

Greg continued down the corridor, monitoring the various checkpoints and making sure that everything looked in order with the surveillance cameras. He had to face facts. He was really hoping to find an excuse to get another peek at the cute girl, Adrianna, who had just started working here. Navigating his way through the facility, he made a few sharp turns, making it to the most restricted and confidential areas. He paused by an area that was owned by the government where they kept highly secured sensitive information. He scanned his ID badge and used a fingerprint scanner to verify his identity before being allowed to pass.

As he walked through the halls, Greg felt a sense of unease. The Limestone Vault was one of the most secure facilities in the country, and the work he did here was of the utmost importance. He knew that any breach of security could have disastrous consequences, both for the facility and for the safety of the people who depended on it. Just like Jeremy said, they had fortified the Limestone Vault like Fort Knox. No one was getting in here.

Despite the seriousness of his work, Greg couldn't help but feel a sense of satisfaction at the end of each day. He knew that the work he did here was making a difference, and that he was helping to protect the people and the country he loved.

After his rounds, he headed back to the entrance of the Vault to run security while another guard did their circuit of the facilities. It was a long afternoon, but he couldn't keep from grinning when he saw Adrianna walking out from the Vault. He'd stayed late, working a bit past when his shift was over, hoping to see her again before he left for the day. He made sure that he placed himself front and center so she would have to ask him to retrieve her cell phone instead of one of the other guards, and he would get a chance to ask about her day.

Greg was thinking of something particularly funny or memorable to say as she walked up, but when his eye caught a bulge under her blazer, all thoughts of humor left his brain. He went into security mode and braced himself for having to bust a new employee for stealing office supplies.

Then the bulge under her jacket moved. Office equipment didn't squirm. Eyes narrowing, Greg tried to figure out what Adrianna was hiding when a small head popped up over the button of her blazer. How in the world did she smuggle a cat in this morning? He spent a lot of time talking with her and running her through security. He must really be off his game to have missed her furry friend.

Greg raised his eyebrow as he seemed to take in the cat, her ruined blazer, and bleeding hand. Adrianna walked up to him and stopped, but before she could say a word, Greg uncharacteristically interrupted her. He was a rule follower to his very core. "Well, it certainly looks like you have had an eventful first day on the job."

He frowned. "You know you're not allowed to bring your pet to work, right? I watched as we screened your bags. How in the world did you smuggle that little guy in?"

Adrianna's cheeks flushed pink. "I found her in the cave. With a bit of food, I was able to coax her out of hiding, but now I have no idea what to do with her. I'm not looking for a pet right now."

Greg's shoulders relaxed, relieved that he hadn't let a cute smile make him sloppy in his job and that she wasn't a thief that he would have to arrest. The cat meowed at him, and he couldn't help but reach down and pet the cat's head, jerking his hand away when he realized how close it had been to her chest. "Well, this guy must be quite the sneak to get in past security. I will have to figure out how he got in tomorrow. Nothing should be able to get in with the amount of security we have here." Greg paused for a moment before continuing, "Although she seems like a sweet cat. If you don't want her, I think I might know a good home for her."

Sighing with relief, the pitch of Adrianna's voice spiked. "Really? Thank you. I am not set up to take in a cat right now."

"Do you mind hanging on another fifteen minutes while I wrap up things here? Then I can take her as a pet for my niece. She will be over the moon to get a cat."

Adrianna nodded. "Sure. I can do that. Thanks for taking her. I'm glad she will go to a pleasant home. I just need to pick up my cellphone from you, too."

Greg nodded his head and headed over to the drawers where they kept personal items that people accidentally brought with them that weren't allowed in the Vault. In the confusion over the cat, he had totally forgotten about her phone. "I was hoping I would see you before I left for the day. I told you I would take care of your phone, and I wanted to be the one to return it to you." He dug through a drawer, pulled out the bag containing her phone, and brought it over to her.

"Here you go. I kept it safe for you all day." Adrianna smiled in gratitude, and he couldn't stop himself from trying to think of other ways he could make her smile. There was just something about her that made Adrianna impossible to get out of his mind. He said goodbye to his coworkers and signed out, then came over to Adrianna.

"Do you want me to take the cat? What happened today? I know you're working in an old Limestone mine, but they told you your job involved paperwork instead of mining, right?" Adrianna took out the cat and handed her to Greg. Luckily, the cat settled right down in his arms. She had no collar or other form of identification, but she was obviously tame.

Adrianna gave a little chuckle as she did her best to straighten out her jacket and wipe some of the cat hair off it. "Yeah, I did lots of paperwork today, just had a little trouble getting the cat out of a hole she was hiding in. I'm glad I got her out of there, but I'm not sure that my new first-day-of-work outfit is going to be salvageable for another day."

They walked up to the parking lot together, but soon had to part ways to reach their vehicles. With Greg's hands full, he said, "Have a good afternoon. Hopefully, I'll run into you again for your second day of work."

He had to listen closely as Adrianna quietly replied, "I hope so too." He watched her walk away to an upper parking lot and then made his way to his own car, planning on how he would give Gabby her new pet. First, he stopped at the local general store and bought some food and a bowl, and then drove to his sister's house.

He rang the doorbell, cat in hand. He expected that his niece, Gabby, would be delighted to meet the new addition to the family. The door opened and his niece Gabby's eyes opened even larger. She let loose a squeal that almost sent the cat running.

Chapter Six: The Case of the Speeding Ticket

A drianna

Adrianna rushed around the one-bedroom cottage she was renting, trying to finish brushing her hair while simultaneously getting dressed. Today she was supposed to be at work extra early to be trained in how to process field investigators' reports. She was excited because she was about to get paid to read people's juiciest and darkest secrets.

Unfortunately, this morning her alarm didn't go off, and now she was going to be late! That was not the impression she wanted to keep making at her new job. Adrenaline rushed through her system, but she really wished she had time to make coffee. Glancing down, she saw the romance novel that laid on the floor next to the blow-up mattress in her bedroom. She hopped over the luggage bag sitting next to it and shook her head. It was a bad idea to stay up so late finishing that book, but she was at the good part and wanted to find out if he got the girl in the end. She was going to be so tired later today.

This weekend she would have to find some basic furniture so the place didn't look so bare. Maybe she would get another plant, too. The place felt so empty, and it would be nice to have another living thing here. She may have had a black thumb, but she had to keep trying to keep something alive, right? Her new cottage demanded it.

There was plenty of beautiful flora outside this quaint little cottage. When she first arrived, the landlord had met her outside. Adrianna looked over the flowers nervously. They were absolutely stunning, but it did not prepare her to care for them. Unfortunately, there really weren't any other places available to rent close by, especially on such short notice. Her landlord had assured her that all she needed to do with them was "let God water them," so she had agreed to try it.

Before this, she was living in the city in a pre-furnished apartment where she paid rent month to month. Her landlord knew she would leave soon, and that she was just waiting for her background investigation to go through. After all that waiting, she had assumed they would give her a start date a few weeks out. When she received her clearances, she got a phone call asking if she could start the following Monday. With only one weekend to move, she was lucky to find this cottage to rent, but hadn't had time for packing more than the bare necessities.

Hopping into the car, Adrianna did a quick inventory to make sure she'd remembered everything. If she hurried and speed walked the entire way from the parking lot to her cubicle, maybe she could still make it. She was a good hard worker, and didn't want to give the impression of being lazy and tardy all the time.

Adrianna's cottage was on the outskirts of a small rustic town called Arcadianville. The opposite of what she was used to. Today she zipped through the back country roads that were mostly empty, trying to make up for lost time. Then she heard the sirens.

With a loud groan, Adrianna pulled her car over and rested her head on her steering wheel. She would never make it now. She heard a light tapping on her window and turned to see none other than Greg, but this time in an officer's uniform.

She put her window down, ducked her head, and looked up at him through her eyelashes. "Hello, Gre... Officer. Are you a police officer who does security at the Vault?"

Greg gave her a small smile. "Why, if it isn't Adrianna? I seem to run into you everywhere, and I never know what to expect when I see you. This town is too small to support a full-time cop, so I work part time. A few hours in the mornings and evenings here and there and a lot over the weekends. Most of my weekdays I spend as a security guard at the Vault."

He cleared his friendly expression, and the smile disappeared. "Do you realize you were going fifty-five in a forty-five mile-per-hour area?"

Adrianna broke eye contact and hung her head. "Yes, I'm sorry. I know it's no excuse, but I was running late for work."

Greg nodded his head. "Well, I happen to be able to give warnings to good Samaritans who go out of their way to save a cat lost in an old limestone mine. Just make sure you're more careful with the speed limits, or I will have to give you a ticket next time. There may not be many people out and about this early, but my nephew, Andrew, delivers papers and is out here on these back roads on his bike, so please be careful."

With a breath of relief, she looked up and smiled as Greg leaned down, arms propped comfortably on her windowsill. "It's his family that I gave the cat to. My sister wasn't too sure at first, but my little niece, Gabby, was beside herself. They named the cat Scarf, and Gabby will take good care of her."

He stood up straight and gently tapped on her car twice. "Well, I'll let you get going to work since you're in such a hurry. I need to go home and change for my security shift that starts in an hour. Maybe I'll see you soaking in the sun at lunch again?"

Adrianna laughed briefly. "Maybe. I really did like spending my lunch stretching my legs and seeing the sunlight for a few minutes after being in that old cave. It's really neat working down there, but also a bit claustrophobic. I just have to make sure this time I don't get lost getting back to my room!"

Moving out of the way, he turned to her car and smiled broadly, letting his dimple show. "I hope your day goes well. Such a special woman like you deserves it!" Then he headed back to his police vehicle. She watched out of her rear-view window as he turned off his lights, backed up and headed back into town.

She would almost think that he was flirting with her sometimes, but she watched him closely while everyone was going through security yesterday morning, and he just seemed to be a genuinely friendly guy. He greeted everyone by name and asked about people's pets and ailing grandparents. It's such a shame that the giant scar was featured so prominently on his face; he was a real catch.

She was much happier reading about people's lives and reducing their issues to letters and numbers than having to deal with all the drama that came with relationships. After dating a few guys and nothing serious came of it, she decided to focus more on her work than on personal relationships. She hated having roommates in college and was now happy to sit in a cubicle by herself most of the day. Her job would be perfect if she didn't miss the sunshine so badly.

Keeping to the speed limit, Adrianna finished her drive to work and made her way as swiftly as she could to her desk. Judy eyed her walking in and gave a humph sound as she stuck her nose in the air. She looked down at her new watch. She was twenty minutes late.

There was a pile of paperwork on her desk and a note from Henrietta. *"I have a doctor's appointment, but should be back later this afternoon. Start reading through these investigations, and we will talk about how to process them tomorrow. Put a post-it note on anything you read that might potentially be an issue in their report."*

Adrianna said a quick prayer for Henrietta and the baby's health and then opened up the first packet of papers. They enthralled her as she entered someone else's world.

Chapter Seven: The Case of the Purple Pool

*A**drianna*

The first man Adrianna read about had admitted to trying to break into his high school when he was seventeen to play a senior prank. He had two large buckets of purple pond dye he was planning on dumping into the school pool. He claimed it was a harmless joke that would have dissipated in a few days. The school wanted to press charges, but since he was under eighteen, he ended up being released to his parents. Adrianna put a post-it on that section to ask Henrietta if it was something that should be in her report or not.

The next person told the interviewer that they had taken no international trips in the past five years and didn't plan to soon. That alone didn't raise any warning flags to Adrianna until she got to an interview from a friend. The friend said that the person being investigated took a yearly trip to Russia. He thought it was to see family or something. She flagged that, too.

She munched on her sandwich while she read over Charles Kent's file. It was pretty straightforward. He had some student loans he was paying off, and his brother said he spent too much time playing video games, but otherwise, he seemed like a really nice guy. He was friendly, loved going to sporting events, and regularly went to karaoke nights. It surprised her to see that he lived only about twenty minutes away from Arcadianville.

Today, she ate her lunch early while reading so she could get the most time outside during her half-hour lunch break. She sped, walking to the cave opening, and looked down at her watch. She calculated she could make it in only seven minutes when she was motivated. Not wanting to spend the rest of her time just standing in the small area between the entrance to the cave and the guardhouse, she went out through security.

There was no sign of Greg, and she found herself oddly disappointed. She had missed him this morning, since she started her shift early, and missed his handsome dimple. That was very nice of him to take that cat off her hands and give her a warning instead of a ticket. *I wonder if there is something nice I can do for him, but what?*

She wasn't exactly the type to bake cookies to bring to someone, and didn't have any local connections. Really, she had no real friends right now. She'd left the few she had behind when she moved to the middle of nowhere. She would keep thinking about it. There had to be something he liked.

Once outside, she took a lap around the parking lot, chuckling at herself for enjoying the feeling of freedom so much. Sometimes being in such a secure facility felt a little like being in prison, not that she would know what that felt like. Way too soon, it was time to go back through security and make her way back down to her cubicle.

Feeling refreshed, she dug into her casework with more fervor. She started reading a thick file about a man who was admitting to everything that had ever happened in his life. Imagining the investigator's face during this interview, she had to stifle a laugh at the next part. He'd admitted to the investigator that he was recently hospitalized to have a metal welding nut removed from around his "manly area."

The last file on her desk to review for today showed a picture of a pretty young woman. Her name was Dana Hemsworth. She hoped she didn't have a horrifying past or get anything stuck in uncomfortable places.

She went through her interview and was a bit taken aback when she read how much she loved to root for her favorite local sports team. One of her friends mentioned that their favorite pastime was to hit karaoke bars together. It sounded oddly familiar. She looked to see where she lived. She was right here in Arcadianville.

She flipped back to the background of the man she was reviewing earlier. He was good-looking and thin. It was a shame these two didn't know each other. She was sure if they just met, they would really hit it off.

A coworker she didn't know came over to her desk, breaking up her train of thought. She talked with her hands as she spoke. "Hello, my name is Cindy. I'm another trainer here at BISS. It's nice to meet you. I should have come over to say hello earlier, but I'm sorry that right now I'm here to be the bringer of bad news."

Adrianna furrowed her brow. "It's nice to meet you, too. What is the bad news?"

Cindy handed her a piece of paper. "Darren said you and that other new employee don't have your e-mail set up and working, and your trainer called in and requested off for the rest of today. I printed a copy of the e-mail for you guys and am passing it along."

After reading over the letter, Adrianna looked back up again when Cindy summarized it for her. "Unfortunately, someone lost a birth certificate. It wasn't in the folder when a reviewer went to finish up someone's case. That's a big security risk, and if we don't find it, we have to report it to the government since this position was for a high-level clearance with them. Anyway, we all have to come in on Saturday and go through the bins of things to be shredded until we find it. Be here at eight. Hopefully, it won't take too long, but don't make any plans for tomorrow, just in case."

There goes my chance to go furniture shopping tomorrow. Cindy moved over and told Judy the same message, and Adrianna watched her hands as they moved. Oddly, a bit of blue ink was on the side of her hand, and her pinky finger had a slight bend to it that seemed familiar.

When Cindy finished speaking, Adrianna got her attention by saying, "Oh, Cindy. I have a question for you. Did you leave me the handprint on my desk yesterday?"

Cindy gave her a big smile. "Looks like we have the employee of the year over here! Good job. We'll make an excellent investigator out of you yet!"

Adrianna smiled as Cindy walked away, and she noticed Judy out of the corner of her eye. Lips pursed into a sour frown, Adrianna wondered if someday they would stick that way. She had a glare that could kill. Adrianna nervously looked away and got back to work on the assignment she had been working on before Cindy had come over with the bad news about tomorrow's task.

A few hours later, it was time for everyone to get off for the day. Adrianna stayed late in order to finish up some work before Saturday's task began. As she made her way out of BISS, questions filled her head:

Why would one single paper require us all being called in? Why does Judy have such a problem with me?

When Adrianna arrived home, all she wanted to do was take a hot bath and forget about everything that had happened today at work. But before she could relax, there was still more work to be done—she had promised herself earlier that day that she would memorize those issue codes so that she wouldn't have to be constantly looking them up and she could work swifter. She spent the rest of the evening memorizing background investigation processing codes. By the time she glanced at her clock, and it shone after midnight brightly, her tired mind was more than ready for some shuteye. She needed to be sharp as she searched through shredding bins come Saturday morning.

Exhausted, Adrianna drifted off to dream about a certain police officer diving into a purple pool to rescue her from a near drowning. He leaned down to perform mouth-to-mouth resuscitation, not realizing that she had already regained her wits.

Chapter Eight:
The Case of
the Missing Birth
Certificate

A *drianna*

Adrianna sat on the hard, cold floor and rummaged through endless papers, skimming over anything that didn't look like a birth certificate and checking the names of the ones that were. Her boss, Darren, gave her an industrial-sized garbage can full of paper that was going to be shredded. He told her to sort through it and look for a single slip of paper that may or may not be in there. It was torture.

Some people were searching through the active cases, while others were looking behind filing cabinets and under desks. No one had it easy, but this was not what she'd pictured her job would be like. They took every detail seriously down here.

Her mind roamed to her day yesterday, reading through people's backgrounds. All the drama, strife, secrets, miscommunication, and inconsistencies. It was all right in front of her. People's whole lives were before her very eyes—truly an open book. It was like one of the romance novels she loved to read, but better, because it was all real and t rue.

Her mind came back to the man and the woman that were so similar, but both claimed to be single on their investigations. She really wished there was something she could do to get them together. It was driving her crazy that she found two people absolutely perfect for one another, and there was nothing she could do about it. It would be unethical to meddle with privileged information.

She was so deep in thought that she realized she had stopped working. She looked up at the mountain of papers and sighed to herself sadly. Her mind whirled a million miles a minute as she continued going through mindless motions. She would never abuse her position of power, but that didn't mean she couldn't daydream.

Like the beginning of a romance novel, both Charles and Dana sat at a hockey game. Totally oblivious of one another, they both stood and cheered on their team, with only an empty seat between them. Dana accidentally knocked her phone onto the floor and Charles reached down to pick it up at the same time as her, causing them to bump heads. They each stumbled over an apology as they looked up and gazed into one another's eyes, now oblivious to the roar of excitement surrounding them...

From somewhere across the room, she heard a voice call out, "I found it!" Adrianna exhaled a breath of relief. She had only been here for a little over two and a half hours. Even with her daydreams of keeping her company, she didn't think she could have survived doing this all day long.

Adrianna cleaned up the shredded mess around her as Henrietta came over to her and Judy, who was nearby, with a similar shredder bin to go through. With her normal smile pinned on her face, she greeted them. "Good morning, ladies. Sorry I wasn't here yesterday, but I will be here bright and early Monday morning to go over everything you found in the investigations I gave you to read over. For today, we're done. You two can go home as soon as we clean everything up."

Before she could leave, Adrianna quickly asked, "How was your doctor's appointment? Just a regular checkup? Is everything alright?"

Henrietta gave her the first strained smile she had seen on the beautiful and cheerful woman's face. "I was having some awful muscle spasms in my leg, so I am going to take it easy, but everything should be fine."

Adrianna may not have liked idle chitchat, but she cared for this cheerful woman and wished her the best. Chewing on her bottom lip, Adrianna looked up, concerned. "Let me know if you need help with anything, okay?"

Henrietta looked at her belly and rubbed it. She stuck out her tongue as she said, "I'm going to eat bananas and ride the bus, but it will all be worth it for this little guy."

After Henrietta left, Adrianna cleaned up the massive number of papers around her and placed them back into the shredder bin. At one point, Henrietta came back and escorted Judy to their boss, Darren's , office. Judy looked scared going in, and a few moments later, she came out of Darren's office crying. She hurriedly grabbed her bag and rushed out the door. *Did she just get fired? Was she the one who lost the birth certificate?*

She picked up the last of her papers, secured the lock on the paper shredder, and then looked at Judy's pile beside her. It looked like her workday wasn't over yet. With an exaggerated sigh, she cleaned up

Judy's mess, too. She couldn't leave it unsecured, so she kept working to avoid making Henrietta do it.

Job completed, she walked out of the Vault, humming to herself. There was no sign of Greg; he was probably off being a police officer somewhere right now. The other guards were friendly enough, but none of them gave her the warm greeting that he did. A part of her wished she could read about his background. While she now knew so many intimate details about complete strangers, this man who was becoming her friend was a mystery.

Looking at her watch, she realized it was still early enough to pick up a few necessities. She got in her car and turned on the cellphone that she now left there whenever she entered the Vault. A quick search showed what she had already guessed. There weren't many shopping options around, although she located a thrift store right in downtown Arcadianville, so that would be her first stop.

After picking up a small two-person kitchen table, an end table, some kitchen supplies, and a small spider plant, she brought her finds into her new home. The cottage was small, containing only one bedroom, a small eat-in kitchen, and a cozy living room, but it woul d suffice for her. She had always been more of a loner. She rarely had people over and worked too much to give proper care to a pet.

The kind man at the thrift store suggested she go to the larger town of Hillsboro, about forty-five minutes away, to find a bed, dresser, and a love seat for the living room. Then her house would be full. Her plans for Sunday afternoon now involved shopping in the "grand metropolis" of Hillsboro and getting lunch in a quaint diner he told her about. She chuckled at herself, wondering if somewhere named Hillsboro would ever feel like a busy place to her.

Glad to fill the rest of her weekend, she thought about next weekend and the one after that. She really didn't know what to do during the rest of her weekends here except sit around at home and read romance novels. In the city, there were museums, street fairs, plays, and a few friends she sometimes met up with at new restaurants every Friday. Here, it was just her... and the plant that she was going to struggle to keep alive.

She placed her spider plant on the windowsill above her sink. It was in direct sunlight, right where it would be easy to remember to water it. She looked at the hardy little plant. For its sake, she hoped she could keep this one alive.

She heard something outside her cottage moving around in the dark. After peering through the windows and not spying anything, she secured all the windows and doors. That night, she crawled into bed with her phone, wishing she could ask a certain police officer to swing by, but not wanting to bother anyone with what was probably just a raccoon.

Chapter Nine: The Case of the Pet Duck

*A*drianna

The next Monday, Judy was sitting at her desk, working away like nothing happened. Adrianna stared at her a moment as she walked to her desk. Part of her wondered if she should go over and ask if she was alright. Another part didn't want to stir the hornet's nest. She left her be for now. The woman looked so absorbed in her work that she might just want to be left alone.

Adrianna sat down at her own desk, getting to work. She wanted to be an expert background investigator, so she had a lot to learn. She had to take extra care to make sure that no detail, however small, was skipped while she waded through someone's life story.

Soon enough, she was so immersed in her work that she almost forgot about Judy. Almost, but not quite. Every once in a while, she would glance over at the other woman and wonder what was going on in her head. There were definitely more questions that needed answering, but she also wanted to make sure the woman was alright, even if Judy probably wouldn't return the favor in the future.

Adrianna waited until lunch to approach Judy. She wanted to be sure that her mind was on her work and not distracted by Judy's drama. Despite her grumbling stomach, Adrianna got up and walked over to Judy's desk.

"Hey, Judy," she said, cautiously. "I just wanted to check in and see how you are doing. I noticed you seemed a bit... off... Saturday. Is everything okay?"

Judy looked up, surprise on her face. She was clearly not expecting Adrianna to be so direct. She hesitated, until finally, she sighed and nodded her head.

"It was nothing, really," she said, her voice shaky. "Just... family issues that I needed to take care of." Adrianna cocked her head and waited for more, surprised not to hear Judy's normal mocking tone.

Adrianna nodded in understanding. She knew family issues could be complicated, and she didn't want to be nosy.

"Well, I just wanted to make sure you were okay," Adrianna said, giving Judy a small smile. "You can talk to me if you need anything."

Judy's gaze moved away, and Adrianna hoped it touched her. Maybe this would be a turning point in their relationship. Even if they weren't ever going to be best friends, it would be nice not to dread speaking with her coworker.

"Thanks," Judy said, her voice softer. "I appreciate it."

Adrianna smiled before getting up to go back to her desk. She was glad that she had taken the time to check in on Judy. Maybe things would be different between them now.

Returning to her desk only to swipe her sandwich, Adrianna started the long haul out of the mines to glimpse sunshine and maybe, if she was lucky, to say hello to Greg. Speed walking all the way, she only stopped to press her body against a cave wall when a large truck sporting the paper shredder's logo drove by.

The first rays of light warmed her body immediately, and it almost seemed like she could feel the vitamin D soaking into her skin. She glanced around and frowned. There was no sign of Greg today. She ate her sandwich in only a few bites before she rushed back down the cave's tunnels. Unfortunately, she didn't have time to enjoy her walk today, but she couldn't bring herself to skip it and risk missing Greg. Did he look for her like she looked for him?

Pushing her disappointment away, her feet moved as her mind wandered to a case she read about this morning. The ex-girlfriend praised her previous lover in his background investigation, gushing over what a great guy he was, and she couldn't help wondering if there was still something between them they could salvage.

She imagined the two of them bumping into one another at a bus stop and catching up while they were waiting. *Missing the easy camaraderie between them, they agree to meet for coffee just for old time's sake...*

Back at her desk, Adrianna shuffled through her papers to work on the next investigation on her pile for the day. It was a thick one, and she wondered if people that told an investigator their entire life story have more issues she needed to flag or fewer? She would soon find out.

She glanced over at Judy. They made eye contact for a second before the woman pointedly ignored her. She wouldn't count on anything coming from that relationship. The only reason she was feeling lonely must be because she wasn't working hard enough. She would ask if she could bring some of her cases home with her to work on during the weekend. Then she wouldn't need to worry about the empty weekends ahead of her, making friends, or seeing Greg again. Digging into the secret lives of strangers was more intriguing than any novel she'd ever read before, and she would typically choose the company of a good book over a person, anyway.

Feeling confident in her plan of future solitude, Adrianna peered over the open file before her, trying to make sense of the man's background and character. He had served in the military, albeit a short tenure, then started his own business, which did okay but not great.

A few unrelated misdemeanors were scattered across his rap sheet that she would have to report, but she was feeling confident that she wouldn't find any serious issues in the background of this run-of-the-mill guy. But then something strange caught her eye, a minor note in bright blue ink by one of the section headers. It read: "Came to interview with pet duck."

Adrianna paused for a moment, completely unsure of how to take this new information. Was this bit of information really necessary? What made someone carry a duck around with them? She shook her head and dived back in to see why he would bring a farm animal to an interview. Maybe he planned on keeping a sheep in his cubicle? She read further into the report and quickly realized why it was included—he brought the duck as a comfort animal who could calm him when he got overwhelmed during the interview process.

The more she read about this man's past relationships, the more she could see why he needed such a companion by his side. There was an instance where his mistress had called 911 after finding him in bed with his wife. She had to read that one twice to make sure she read it right. There were accounts of cheating on girlfriends and living beyond his means while failing to pay off debts; all followed by stories of running away, leaving debts unpaid, and employers unsatisfied. He certainly seemed like someone who needed comfort during difficult times—especially when being questioned about shady behaviors from his past.

Adrianna finished up reading the report on the man, but still couldn't shake off the memory of imagining him accompanied by a pet duck at his interview. It would have been an odd sight, but she found the medical note saying that his support duck could accompany him. Deciding not to assign an issue number to the duck, she easily found enough issues in his other misdeeds that she knew he would get a close review before being awarded or denied any kind of clearance.

Adrianna smiled to herself as she imagined the day when she would get promoted to being an interviewer, having the opportunity to ask all of these questions, and hearing all of this firsthand. Yes, it would mean talking to people all day, but she couldn't imagine a more interesting job, traveling the country to track down all the juiciest details of someone's past. She looked around her little cubicle and opened up her laptop, writing any potential clearance risks.

She was made for this work. The more she read, she realized she knew more about most of these people than their closest family and friends. *Who needs deep relationships, anyway?* She had one of the most interesting jobs there was. Besides, she got a spider plant. She wouldn't be lonely in her cottage anymore.

Chapter Ten: The Case of the Baby Gift

*A*drianna

After asking Henrietta how to code a prank where water balloons were dropped on unsuspecting customers from a rooftop, Adrianna turned to head back to her desk. Before she could leave, Henrietta frowned as she looked up at Adrianna. "You know, you don't have to work twelve-hour days, right? There will always be more cases to process. I mean, you have shown an amazing work ethic, but you can have a life too."

Twiddling her fingers, Adrianna admitted, "Yeah, I know, but I really enjoy this work and want to make a good impression. I also just moved here and have nothing else going on, so I might as well get up to speed at work as fast as I can."

Henrietta raised her eyebrows in surprise. "Many people who work here commute from all over. We're a small town, and some people commute an hour to an hour and a half to get here every day. Are you telling me you live right by here and you never told me? Where are you staying?"

Adrianna hesitated before answering. "Um, I'm renting a little cottage on Bough Street. It has a little flower garden in the front."

Henrietta smiled, her eyes crinkling at the corners. "Oh, that place is lovely! You should have told me sooner. We could carpool! That's only about five minutes from my little hobby farm."

Henrietta picked up a pen and a blank post-it note. "That settles it. My husband and I are having a BBQ this weekend to celebrate the baby coming. A lot of our neighbors will be there, and you can come and meet some people."

Shrugging her shoulders, Adrianna tried to argue by saying, "Well, actually, I'm not really a big crowd person..."

Henrietta waved her hand dismissively. "Oh, nonsense! Come. It will be fun! Plus, it will give you a chance to meet some people in town. My husband and I have been here for years, so we know everyone."

Henrietta wrote an address, a date, and a time, and held it in front of Adrianna. Adrianna hesitated before taking the scrap of paper. Henrietta looked her in the eye. "You really need to be there. You told me to tell you if I needed anything, and what I need is for you to come to my party." She smiled widely, showing off her perfectly white teeth. "I'll be expecting you!"

"Okay," Adrianna said finally, after a few moments of contemplation. "I'll come."

Adrianna took the post-it and walked back to her desk. She wasn't particularly pleased about being strong-armed into going to the party, but she was warming up to the idea. Now she had something to do next weekend other than talking to her spider plant. Was it weird that she was thinking of naming it Greg?

Maybe she could show up for a short bit to express her support of Henrietta and then head back home. She was dying to read the stack of new romance novels that had caught her eye while she was waiting in line at the general store, picking up groceries.

As the hours passed, Adrianna grew more and more nervous about the upcoming BBQ. She had never been good in social settings, and she wasn't sure what exactly she should wear or what conversations she should have. After all, a lot of people she didn't know were going to be there.

Suddenly, she realized this wasn't just any social event, but also a celebration of a new baby. She needed to find a meaningful gift, and quickly. What could she find out here in the middle of nowhere that would be appropriate?

Hopping into her car, she headed toward Hillsboro to shop at the biggest store there. Adrianna put the swaddling blankets and elephant teether into a shopping cart as she wandered around the store. There were so many baby things to choose from, and she felt overwhelmed. She didn't know what things Henrietta needed, but she wanted to get something special for the woman who had been so kind to her and her new little one.

As she walked around the aisle, something caught her eye. It was a beautiful wooden rocking chair with intricate wood carvings adorning the armrests. Adrianna couldn't help but run her fingers along it as she walked past.

She considered purchasing it for a moment until she saw the price tag. She shook her head and smiled as she realized what an extravagant gift it would be, even if Henrietta was her only friend around here. Adrianna grabbed a few more items just in case before heading to the checkout line.

On her way home from Hillsboro, Adrianna noticed that there was an antique store near the highway exit for Bough Street; it was called Letitia's Treasures. She made a detour and stopped on an impulse before continuing home.

The moment Adrianna stepped inside, she could feel the magical atmosphere of Letitia's Treasures pull her in like a magnet; every item seemed to have its own magical story behind it—books filled with stories written by unknown authors that seemed timeless, porcelain dolls with bright eyes and long dresses placed carefully in their glass cases. They almost seemed alive...

Adrianna went directly toward a child-sized wooden rocking chair that looked inviting. Upon closer inspection, Adrianna could see that it wasn't just any rocking chair; this one had carved armrests. While not the same pattern, it had a similar feel to the rocking chair she had seen at the store earlier... only this one was much closer to her price range.

She paid, then using both her arms, she heaved the chair out to her car and sat it down on the ground, only now realizing her mistake. She was so excited about her find that she hadn't taken a moment to think about its size and measure it. While it wasn't full-sized, her car was small, and someone had built this chair solidly. How in the world would she get this home and then to the party tomorrow?

Chapter Eleven: The Case of the BBQ Mission

*A**drianna*

Adrianna's stomach felt jittery as she rode down the dirt road to Henrietta's house. The fact that it was just a casual backyard BBQ and no one would make a big deal out of her being there reassured Adrianna about attending the party.

Adrianna pulled up to a modest-looking house with a small barn in the distance and several cars already parked in the driveway. Taking a deep breath, she grabbed her purse and walked up to the front door.

Once inside, a large man took her hand and shook it vigorously, greeting Adrianna. "Welcome! Henrietta told us a new coworker of hers was going to stop by. I'm so glad you could make it. I'm Henrietta's father, but you can call me Jack."

He quickly introduced Adrianna to several of their friends and family members who had also come to visit. She nodded, unable to remember more than a few of the names that rattled off his tongue. She felt so uncomfortable around all these strangers that all she could think about was how fast she could leave.

He led her to a sliding glass door that opened to the party in the backyard. "Henrietta is out there mingling. Make yourself at home. Food will be ready in about ten minutes. Thanks again for coming. I know it means a lot to Henrietta." With a flash of a smile, he disappeared into the crowd, and Adrianna had no choice but to follow.

Looking around nervously, Adrianna stared at the crowd of strangers and clung onto the gift bag she brought a little tighter. She was now regretting that she had a rocking chair half hanging out of her trunk. The last thing she wanted was to get it out and awkwardly carry it to the gift table in front of these people.

The air was filled with the scent of grilled meat and smoked sausages, mingling with the sweet aroma of freshly baked cakes and pies that made Adrianna's mouth water.

There were blue balloons shaped into an arch, and blue tablecloths upon a few picnic tables sitting on the far side of the yard. At least a dozen kids were running around, zigzagging through the adults.

What have I gotten myself into? Despite her hunger, Adrianna decided to get in, hand over the gift she held, and then she could get out. She would simply leave the rocking chair on their front stoop as a surprise to be found later. Adrianna squared her jaw. She handled sensitive information all the time. She could handle a simple co-ed baby shower.

Finally, she spotted Henrietta in a cute, tight-fitting blue dress that accentuated her bump. She was standing next to a handsome man with dark skin and curly hair, and the two were laughing in the middle of a group of people.

Trying to ease her anxiety about the crowd, she turned the situation into a game. Her mission was to deliver this parcel no matter what neighborly obstacles were thrown in her way. Her target: Henrietta. An easy enough goal to spot, but not an easy one to attain. Her job, if she chose to accept it, was to deliver this gift to the target while avoiding as many neighbor "mines" as possible.

Plan A: obtain a decoy. Adrianna decided that the easiest way to move through the crowd without looking awkward was to get a drink. She eased her way along the outskirt of the crowd to some drink coolers sitting on the lawn. Her plan was to sip on a soda while nonchalantly working her way through her neighbors. She would look busy, so no one would bother her. Henrietta was busy hosting, so Adrianna would just gently tap her on the shoulder and tell her she just wanted to drop off this gift before she left. Easy-peasy.

Once she accomplished her mission, she would head to her cozy cottage and the romance novel awaiting her. Her mouth watered. She was hungry. Maybe she would bake some cookies so that her stomach would forgive her for not tasting that delicious-smelling barbecue.

She moved through the crowd stealthily, and no one more than glanced her way. Her plan was working perfectly. There wouldn't even be a need for a Plan B. Out of the corner of her eye, she caught sight of someone familiar. At first, she couldn't place her, because she didn't look exactly like the picture in her file, but it was definitely her. Dana Hemsworth, the woman she had read about and thought would be the perfect match for another case file she analyzed.

Panicking, Adrianna detoured away from Dana, unwilling to make small talk with someone whose deepest, darkest secrets she knew. She was determined to keep all the privileged information she obtained for her job locked up tight, but what if she slipped? That woman would think she was a stalker if she accidentally let on that she knew she loved sports and karaoke.

Distracted, she didn't even realize she was walking straight into the side of a tall, muscular man, accidentally spilling her soda all down the front of his gray tight-fitting T-shirt. Mortified, all she could do was stare as the man turned around, and she saw the wide-eyed face of Greg looking back at her.

Abort mission!

Chapter Twelve: The Case of the Spilled Milk

*A*drianna

She wanted to crawl under a rock as the neighboring group of people turned and stared to see what the commotion was. To her dismay, Greg got a gigantic smile on his face. "You know, you could have just said hello. I haven't spilled a drink on a girl I liked since elementary school. Although in that case, it was milk."

Adrianna's face turned red. *How do I respond to that?*

Luckily, Henrietta walked over and saved the day. "Hello, Adrianna! I'm so glad you could make it! I see you already found Greg, from the Vault. Let me introduce you to a few of our other neighbors that work down there."

Then Henrietta eyed Greg. "What have you been doing to get so messy?"

Finally piping up, Adrianna grimaced as she explained, "I'm so sorry. I spilled my soda all over him. Henrietta, do you have a towel or something I could give him to clean himself up?"

Giving an exaggerated sigh, Henrietta playfully rolled her eyes. "Yes, follow me. If you two children are done goofing off, then you can get cleaned up."

Greg and Adrianna followed her into the house. Adrianna only now realized that she really didn't need to be there. Henrietta was more than capable of giving Greg a towel, and he was more than capable of cleaning himself up. She was just an extra person. *Could I get any more awkward?*

Adrianna stepped backwards toward the door. "I'm sorry again about the shirt, but since Henrietta is now..."

Henrietta walked into the room with a towel and threw it at Greg, interrupting what Adrianna was saying. Greg caught it easily and tried to dry up his shirt. Adrianna stood there awkwardly, not knowing if she should stay or bolt. If she left, where would she go? She hadn't delivered her present yet, and she didn't know anyone else here. She needed to come up with a Plan B fast because Plan A had gone up in flames.

Henrietta said, "Here, give me your shirt. I'll throw it in the dryer for a few minutes and you'll be almost as good as new."

Bunching up the bottom of his shirt, he easily pulled it off and threw it at Henrietta. Adrianna couldn't help gape at the muscular abs standing in front of her and the low-riding pants that showed trimly sculpted muscles around the rim of his pants. Apparently, Henrietta must have caught her gaping, because she heard a soft chuckle as the woman walked away, presumably to dry the shirt.

Greg turned to her. "Do you mind waiting with me a bit while I wait for my shirt to dry? I can't go out there like this, and I can't expect

Henrietta to stay in here with me at her party. I'm surprised to see you here. Do you live nearby?"

Adrianna tried to focus her gaze on his face, but her eyes seemed to have a mind of their own as they slowly slid back down his rock-hard body. She cleared her throat and just looked down at her hands. They were safe. "Yes, I'm renting a cottage right down the road, on Bough Street."

She heard the pitch of his voice raise as if it impressed him. "Wow, there are some beautiful flowers outside that place. You must be great with a garden."

Shuffling her feet, Adrianna looked back up at him with a half-smile. "Actually, I'm terrified that I'm going to kill all of my landlord's plants. I'm horrible with them."

Greg cocked his head and hooked one of his hands into his jeans pocket. "My mom always had a flower garden while we were growing up. If you want, I can stop by and show you how to weed and water them."

Nodding, Adrianna gave him a full smile. He was such a nice guy that he would probably offer to help anyone with their flowerbeds, right? "That would be great, thanks."

Henrietta came back out with Greg's t-shirt. It still smelled faintly of her cola and had a bit of a watermark, but at least it was dry. "Here, this will have to do for the rest of the party. Unfortunately, you won't fit into any of Bill's shirts."

Turning to Adrianna, Henrietta continued, "Speaking of Bill, Adrianna, I have to introduce you to my husband. Come on." Henrietta took Adrianna's hand and pulled her outside, with Greg following close behind.

Adrianna held up the present that she had been holding. "Oh, that would be great. I just want to give you this before I forget. I got you a little something for the baby." *There, mission accomplished.* She may not have done it stealthily or skillfully, but she was done. Now she could drop off the rocking chair and escape the next chance she got.

They stopped right outside the door. Opening up the bag and pulling out the gifts, Henrietta oohed and ahhed for a few moments. "Thank you so much for this. You didn't have to bring anything."

Smiling, Adrianna assured her, "I wanted to do something. You have been so nice to me since I started working at BISS and living here. It's the least I could do. Please let me know if you need anything. I'm right down the road."

Adrianna caught sight of Dana walking by in the crowd. She couldn't help wondering if the woman was here with anyone special. If she could only meet that guy she read about, Charles, she was sure they would hit it off. She avoided eye contact. It would simply be too weird to introduce herself and talk to the woman.

Although the details were fading with time and reading the backgrounds of many more people, she knew too many intimate details about that woman's life, and she couldn't share them with anyone, not even the subject being investigated. The woman could submit for a copy of her background to see what the investigator wrote up about her and her own notes on her investigation, but not until after her background investigation was totally complete.

She looked back at Henrietta to see a calculating quirk to her eyebrows as a smile crossed her face. "Well, there is actually one thing I need you to do for me. It would really set my mind at ease with the baby."

Nodding her head cautiously, Adrianna remembered the last time Henrietta took her up on her offer. She listened carefully to what her next mission would entail. "Sure. What can I do for you?"

Pointing to Greg, she said, "I need you to go out with this big lug. It will keep him busy, so he'll stop pestering me about how I'm feeling." Adrianna had walked right into that one and only had herself to blame.

Chapter Thirteen: The Case of the Failed Set-Up

G^{reg}

His stomach knotted up when Henrietta mentioned a date. Especially a date with *this* woman. He found Adrianna funny and attractive, and he never knew when he would run into her or what she would be up to. He looked forward to their brief run-ins, even if he did get covered in soda.

The only problem was, he hadn't asked a girl out since the accident. During his high school days, he was quite popular and earned the distinction of being voted as the most attractive in his yearbook. He was such a jerk back in those days. He thought he had it all until he lost it.

He actually knew Henrietta from the local high school. She had married her high school sweetheart, and they were now having their first baby. On the day he met Adrianna, he had noticed her reaction to his scar. He didn't want her to go on a pity date with him. That scar doomed him to spend the rest of his days alone. He had come to terms with it long ago, but it still stung when that someone was Adrianna.

Oh well, that was why he threw himself into work. He wanted to be a police officer and keep others safe so they didn't make the same mistakes he did. He worked as a security guard at the Vault while he trained to become a police officer, but he loved it there and couldn't bring himself to leave, even when he was offered a job as a full-time cop out of town. Since this was the only place he had ever lived and his friends and family were all right here, he had decided to stay.

When a part-time position opened up here as a police officer, he jumped at the opportunity. He worked full-time in security and part-time as an officer. He felt good about making a difference in his community and keeping people safe, and all the hours kept him from feeling too lonely in his forced life of bachelorhood.

He waited for a second to hear what Adrianna would say to Henrietta trying to be a matchmaker, but she stood there, eyes wide like a deer caught in headlights. What if she only agreed to go out with him out of pity? From the look on her face, he thought a date had probably never occurred to her until Henrietta put her on the spot.

The only date he was on in the last few years was a woman who had asked him out. He had been excited. She was nice. That just made the letdown twice as a bad when he found out that she only asked him out because she viewed him as some sort of charity case.

He liked Adrianna too much and couldn't stand to hear her turn him down in front of everyone. He chickened out of hearing her reply and decided to be proactive, so Henrietta didn't meddle again.

Greg stretched and scratched the back of his neck. "Actually, I have a lot going on working two jobs right now, so I'm not really looking to date anyone. If you are looking for a friend, though, I'm happy to share a table over a cup of coffee."

Adrianna smiled tentatively and nodded. "That sounds nice. I'd like that," she said, her voice barely above a whisper. Was she relieved that he hadn't asked her on a date or happy for the chance to spend time with him? Despite the awkwardness of the set-up, he looked forward to some time alone with her.

Greg smiled too and said, "Great. Are you free on Monday evening? My shift ends at seven, so we could grab something casual, like decaf coffee, if you're interested."

Giving him a slight smile, Adrianna simply said, "Sure." He was having a really hard time reading this quiet woman. If she wouldn't say much, he at least wished he could read her mind. Was she quiet because she didn't want to get coffee with him, or quiet because she was relieved she didn't have to go on an actual date with him?

He raised his eyebrows questioningly and watched her features for any signs of what she was feeling. "Can I pick you up at 7:30?"

Adrianna nodded, but Greg saw her eyes were on a woman walking toward them. One of their neighbors, Dana, walked over and joined them. Henrietta smiled and pointed to Adrianna. "Dana! So nice of you to join us. I would like you to meet our new neighbor, Adrianna."

Dana gave a bright smile and held out her hand. "Very nice to meet you. The people around here are so kind, I'm sure you will like it."

Stiffly, Adrianna held out her hand and shook Dana's. "So nice to... meet you too."

Adrianna shifted from one foot to the other and looked quite uncomfortable, like when she first arrived. He had spied her across the crowds of well-wishers and was going to go over and say hello, but then she set off like a woman on a mission, at least until she spilled her drink all over him.

She clutched her purse to herself. "Well, I need to get home and… water my plant. Thank you so much for inviting me, Henrietta. I just have something I need to drop off on your porch for you, and then I think I'll be on my way."

Smiling, Henrietta gave her a side hug, to leave room for her enormous belly. "Thanks so much for stopping by. What could be in your car? The baby gift was already so thoughtful. Here, why doesn't Greg help you fetch it while I make you a plate to take home? It doesn't look like you had anything to eat, and it's coming off the grill fresh right now."

Adrianna hurried away without another word. He soon followed with a plate of food. She was a woman of few words and didn't seem the most comfortable in crowds. Not too long after she arrived, Adrianna was already ready to leave. She had shown up, left a gift, and escaped the first opportunity she got. He loved interacting with people, but he guessed it took a different kind of person to go willingly into a cave and stare at a computer all day long.

He saw her struggling to pull a child-sized rocking chair out of the backseat of a small hatchback. She'd wedged it in awkwardly so that it hung partly out the window. He hurried over. "Here, let me get that for you. Is this a tiny rocking chair? I think Henrietta will love this when you bring it in to her."

Greg handed her the plate and then moved the chair back and forth until it came free of the car. Adrianna cocked her head and raised an eyebrow at him in a way that made him feel like she wanted something from him. If it was within his capabilities, it was hers.

"Actually, I was hoping you could take it in for me. I'm going to head home."

"It must be really thirsty."

Adrianna frowned in confusion.

"I mean the plant. It's lucky, having you take such good care of it."

Adrianna chewed on her lip for a moment. "I promised it I would keep it alive, so I, umm... yeah, I better get back to it." Adrianna walked around to the driver's side of her car while he stood holding the small chair.

He watched her drive away and then went back to the party, setting the rocking chair down directly in front of Henrietta. She gasped. "That's so adorable! Is that what Adrianna had in her trunk? Where in the world did she find it?"

Greg shrugged. "I don't know. She said little about it. Just took off in a hurry to water that very thirsty plant of hers."

Henrietta reached into a cooler near their feet and handed him another drink. "So, you and Adrianna... I could practically see the chemistry between the two of you. I don't think you took your eyes off her all night. Why didn't you want to take her on a date? She's a sweet girl."

With a wave of his hand and a shake of his head, he felt like he was tripping over his words in order to set her straight. "No, it's not like that. We barely know each other. She's nice, and I know you meant well trying to set us up, but you don't have to do that. I'm fine. I'm not looking to date right now. It'll be fun to spend some time with her, but it will be as friends, that's all."

Raising her eyebrows, Henrietta moved closer to him so that only he could hear her. "I think you just made up a list of excuses as they rolled off your tongue. Fine, suit yourself. I'll butt out, but if you think she's only interested in you as a friend, then you missed her checking you out when you had your shirt off."

Is it true? Could she be interested in being more than just friends? He shook his head.

His bare chest wasn't the same thing as his scarred face. He wasn't interested in just having a fling, and besides, he didn't think his heart could handle an intimate relationship with Adrianna that meant nothing more to her than just a fun time. They would just have to stay friends. His face was not something that a woman could love, was it?

Chapter Fourteen: The Case of the Fallout Shelter

*A*drianna

Adrianna spent the next morning enthralled in her case-work. The man she was reading about had admitted openly to spending his summers on nude beaches. Normally, one would think that would make good blackmail material. In this man's case, it was something he did regularly with his wife and friends and had no problem sharing about his experiences with his family and associates.

Interviews with several friends and his wife all confirmed that he regularly went to nudist beaches and none of them seemed to think it was weird at all. You couldn't be blackmailed for something you didn't keep a secret.

A loud alarm went off, making Adrianna jump in her seat. A light flashed near the front door, and everyone seemed to leave their stuff, get up, and line up in front of the door. No one seemed too worried, so Adrianna did the same.

She tapped Henrietta's shoulder, who was standing in front of her. "Hey, what's going on?"

The line in front of them moved out the door, and Henrietta took a step back to walk next to Adrianna. Everyone scanned their badges as they left and then moved as a large column down the mine's tunnels. Lots of people were talking as they walked, but Henrietta moved closer and murmured, "We're doing an emergency drill. You will soon find that we do them randomly every few months."

Furrowing her brow, Adrianna asked, "What kind of emergency are we planning for?"

Whispering almost conspiratorially, she answered, "Well, they claim it's for in case of a fire or earthquake, but I've heard that the Limestone Vault is an emergency location that the president himself may come to in the case of a bombing. You'll see when we get there where the emergency shelter is. I've never been inside, but I hear that it's equipped with beds, showers, and enough food to last years for several hundred people down here. There's even supposed to be an underground lake down here somewhere, but I'm not sure where that is."

Letting go and looking around, Adrianna responded, "Thanks for filling me in. This place is fascinating."

Everyone stayed in a roughly two- to four-person column as they leisurely walked past many tunnels deeper into the mines. There was an intersection where she saw Greg directing traffic, but he was much too busy to see her. At one point, they passed a full-sized fire truck parked against a cave wall. Another area had large digging equipment and a dump truck.

The deeper they walked, the more unfinished the cave walls looked. At first, there were rooms and doorways that looked like they were still under construction, but eventually, the walls were their natural gray, and there were no doors in sight. She did not know where they were.

After about twenty minutes, they stopped outside a giant door that had a circular vault door like in a bank. Henrietta pointed. "That's why this place is called the Limestone Vault. As I said, I've never been in there, but I think that's how you would survive a zombie apocalypse."

Adrianna wondered if Greg had ever been in there. When they went on their outing, that wasn't a date tonight, she would have to ask him what it really looked like inside, and if there was any truth to the underground lakes and emergency room.

She was both excited and nervous about going to dinner with him. He was adamant that he only wanted to be friends, so she would respect that. She was really starting to like him and his charming dimple. So what if he had a little scar on his face? Now that she was getting to know the kind man underneath, she barely noticed it anymore.

They all stood around for about five minutes in what seemed like a random tunnel, and then the group moved back the way they'd come. When Henrietta moved, Adrianna followed. Frowning, Adrianna nudged her. "Is that really it? Nothing happens and they say nothing after having us walk all the way down into the belly of this monster of a cave?"

Shrugging, Henrietta stopped, leaned over as best she could, and rubbed one of her calves. "Nope, that's it. Once you do this a few times, you kind of get to know which way to go to get here, but I like to think of it as being paid to go on a nice little walk for an hour. Although, I don't know if I can handle a lot more of these in my current state. These hard cement floors are just killing my poor calves."

Judy walked by, pleasantly talking with a small group of men and women. Hopefully, if she made some friends, then she would be more congenial. Adrianna didn't interact with Judy too much now that their initial training was over, but whenever she did, the woman always said something that set her on edge. She knew she wasn't the most social person, but she still didn't know why things started out so hostile between them.

When they used their badges to log back into their room, some people stood around chitchatting and others took a bathroom break. It was a good fifteen to twenty minutes before everyone got back to work.

Sitting at her desk, Adrianna tried to get back into the case file, but had lost her place when she'd jumped up in surprise at the alarm. *That was the oddest fire drill I have ever taken part in. This place is full of surprises.*

Finding where she left off, she read: "*I wear a speedo in the car to the beach and the parking lot, but once I pass that invisible barrier, everything comes off. It's so much more enjoyable to be at the beach naked than worrying about pesky sand, causing your bathing suit to chafe or leave tan lines. Naked is better.*"

Adrianna marked it as a three for it being a potential blackmail type of issue and an "A" to show that it was minor. Her job was just to find potential problems. She would leave it up to the reviewer to decide if this was something that should be worried about for this person's clearances.

She moved onto the next case. Everything looked perfectly normal until she read about the man trying to save his cat. Climbing the tree to save his scared cat, the man himself got too scared and spent the night stuck in his neighbor's tree. The neighbor spotted him in the middle of the night and called the police...

Chapter Fifteen: The Case of the Bee Sting

A	*drianna*

Dressed in a simple T-shirt and jeans, Adrianna sat on her front porch swing, admiring the surrounding flowers. A small bumble bee buzzed around a purple flower and moved onto the next, with yellow pollen sticking to his feet. *I wonder what type of flower that is? It's really beautiful.*

She was waiting for Greg to pick her up after his shift. While Henrietta surprised her by trying to play matchmaker, Adrianna's pause didn't mean she would have said no. She really liked Greg, and was quite disappointed to hear him find excuses not to go out with her. It was alright; he didn't have to be interested in her that way. They could just be friends like he suggested.

Even though it wasn't an actual date, she was so excited that she got ready early and now was waiting alone with only her thoughts and a bumblebee for company. A car pulled into the driveway, and Greg hopped out. She looked down at the watch that she was now getting used to wearing all the time. He was right on time.

They soon took off toward the "city" of Hillsboro. Greg wore another plain T-shirt that fit tightly across his muscular chest. He turned his head toward her slightly so that he could talk to her while he watched the road. His enormous grin put her at ease. "So, I thought I would update you on how the cat you found is doing. My niece ended up naming her Scarf, instead of the typical cat name Mittens, because the cat likes to sprawl across the back of Gabby's neck like a scarf every time she sits down. I think it looks very uncomfortable, but the two of them are pleased, so who am I to disagree?"

Adrianna chuckled as Greg started to tell her about the mischief that Gabby and Scarf were getting into together. She was glad Greg was carrying the conversation. She'd never been very good at small talk. Before long, they were in Hillsboro. They parked in front of the town's only cafe that was on the corner of a small hockey stadium where the local team, the Honeybees, played.

As she walked up to the entrance of the Honeybee Cafe, she spotted a man and a woman standing in front of a sign that read: "Sting Like a Bee." Upon closer inspection, she realized she was looking at the local man whose background check she'd finished working on a few weeks earlier. Charles. None other than the man she wanted to set up with Dana, but couldn't because of privacy restrictions.

A woman was yelling at Charles. "That's it! I'm tired of you dragging me to these stupid games. I told you I wanted to go on a fancy date tonight, but instead of taking me somewhere fancy, you brought me to yet another game. Well, I'm done." Storming out the door, she left Charles standing there with his back hunched slightly and a large frown on his face. He looked deflated.

Greg leaned over and whispered to her, "Doesn't look like that guy's having too good of a night."

Nodding her head, she walked out the door right behind Greg. "Yeah, what a shame. He looks like a nice clean-cut guy, too. I guess he just didn't find the right woman." Even though she knew there was nothing she could ethically do to get the now-single Charles together with the woman she'd deemed perfect for him, she couldn't stop her mind from running through ideas to get Dana and Charles together. Just to see if there was a spark.

Her mind was so busy that Greg had to nudge her as he repeated, "What would you like to drink? Do you want anything to eat too?"

Adrianna looked around, realizing they were next in line. "Umm... I guess I'll have a decaf tea, no sugar. That should be good."

Adrianna craned her neck around, trying to see if Charles was still outside being shouted at, until she noticed Greg silently watching her with a cocked head. Her cheeks burned. The poor man. Greg was trying, but she'd barely said a handful of words to him tonight. He probably thought she was bored and couldn't wait to leave, which was the furthest thing from the truth. She really wished she had looked up a list of conversation starters on the internet instead of watching the flowers before he picked her up.

A server sat two cups on the counter in front of them, and Greg scooped them up. He carried them to a nearby two-person table, sat the drinks down, and plopped into one of the chairs.

Greg leaned back in his chair and slowly sipped at his drink. "Look at me, blabbering on. That's not what friends do. Why don't you tell me a bit more about yourself? What have you been doing for fun when you're off work?"

Hiding behind her cup, Adrianna sipped her tea. It was scalding her tongue, but she kept drinking little bits so she seemed busy. "Not much. There really isn't much else going on around here that I've seen."

Looking over at her, Greg gave her an enormous smile. "That's just because you don't know where to look. Things to do aren't labeled on a nice neon sign out here, like in your big city. What we have are some spectacular trails and a high biodiversity of wildlife. There's a river nearby that folks like to tube and canoe down, and of course there's fishing and swimming there as well."

Scratching his chin, he seemed like he was having a hard time coming up with lots of activities, too. "We have local events going on pretty regularly, like weddings or Henrietta's baby shower. Whatever the milestone, there is always a good reason to have a party. Sometimes, when things are quiet for a while, someone will host a bonfire just to get together and chitchat. Or there is always deer spotting or cow tipping."

An image of Greg trying to push over a giant heifer popped into her head. "I don't even know what all of those things are. I've gone swimming in a pool. That's about as close to your list as I get. Deer spotting? You're pulling my leg, aren't you?"

He laughed. "Nope, it's a real thing. Deer spotting is something our teens usually do for a hot date, or hunters do it illegally. All you do is park near a field at dusk, and after a few deer enter the field to graze, you catch them in the headlights of your car, making them freeze in place. Just for the record, I don't actually recommend cow tipping either, because it's illegal, impossible for a single person, and can hurt the cow."

Adrianna shook her head. "I'll keep that in mind. No cow tipping. It's like a whole new world in the country. Although, I have to admit, it is more beautiful out here than I ever imagined."

Cow tipping seemed to break the ice. While Greg still carried on a good portion of the conversation, it was becoming more comfortable. Adrianna opened up more than ever before. He probably didn't notice because she still said little, but it was a stretch for her, nonetheless.

Finishing up the last of her tea, Adrianna wasn't ready for the night to end when she was just warming up. It took all of her courage to ask, "You know what, I'm feeling rather peckish. Would you like to grab something to eat with me, as friends?"

Chapter Sixteen: The Case of the Suspicious Diners

Adrianna

Greg took her onto the highway that led back to Arcadianville, and he stopped at a small dingy-looking diner called Buck's Diner. "Since you're new here, I thought you might want to try out our one and only truly local restaurant. They also do takeout. Sometimes I like to call in and order something to-go on a night when I have to work late and don't feel like cooking." He smiled at her as they entered the door. "They have my to-go order memorized."

"I'll keep that in mind," she assured him. It honestly was a pleasant idea. Some nights when she's worked late, she had missed all the city's options to stop and pick up fast food or Chinese takeout on her way home. This might be a nice substitute. Although, she would soon see if the food was any good.

Adrianna looked around at the red-and-white pleather booths. Each table had placemats covering it with ads from local business-es. A metal napkin holder, bottle of ketchup, and a salt and pepper shaker sat on every table. She felt like she'd gone back in time to a nineteen-fifties diner.

There were a handful of other patrons in the restaurant. They nodded their heads in greeting toward Greg and eyed her up. A pretty server with short blonde hair came over to greet them. She gave Greg a big hug. "It's great to see you!" When she spotted Adrianna, her eyes looked her over from head to toe, making Adrianna want to squirm.

Greg seemed to see the two women eying each other, so he started introductions. "Adrianna, this is my sister, Beverly. Bev, I'd like you to meet Adrianna. She works at the Vault with me. She's the one who found Scarf."

With a smile only about half the size of the one she recently gave her brother, Bev reached out her hand and shook Adrianna's. "Nice to meet you, Adrianna. Greg has had only good things to say about you, and my daughter, Gabby, is so in love with that cat. I look forward to getting to know you better." She looked pointedly at her brother.

Either Greg ignored her or Adrianna missed the rest of their subtle exchange, but it definitely put her on edge. His sister wasn't acting hostile, but Adrianna just felt like she was the awkward social outsider again and wished they had stopped at coffee.

Beverly waved her hand toward the tables. "Go ahead and find a seat. I will be right with you guys to take your order." She punched her brother's arm playfully. "I was in a pie-baking mood this morning and baked too much, so dessert's on me."

Greg led her to a table near the back of the room. Everyone they walked past either nodded their head at him or greeted him by name. Adrianna gave a sigh of relief when they finally made it to their own table. When she sat down, she didn't realize that she'd automatically slunk down slightly on her side of the booth. "Wow, you're like a celebrity in here. You should have warned me."

He rubbed the back of his neck. "Yeah, I didn't think about it from your perspective. This is just what happens since I've lived here in such a small community my whole life. I am also the local police officer, always saving someone's runaway dog and looking in on people's houses while they're away on vacation, so they want to make sure that I know they appreciate me. We should have gotten something to eat in the big city of Hillsboro while we were there."

She held up her hands in defense. Maybe it was worth the awkward situation in order to spend more time with such an amazing guy who kept the local area secure and saved puppies for a living. "No, it's okay. I do want to try this place out anyway. Takeout on a busy night, sounds like quite a convenience out here."

They ordered some simple burgers and fries. The food was good, although nothing spectacular. She decided it would still work to feed her in a pinch, and it wasn't like she had any other options.

Now that she had Greg's undivided attention and felt comfortable enough to ask, Adrianna brought up the emergency drill. "So, what exactly was that fire drill thing we did this morning?"

He sat up straight, as if a little surprised at her sudden change in conversation. "Oh, that's something we do every few months to make sure that all personnel working in the Vault know what to do in the case of an emergency. We generally evacuate individual rooms to inside the Vault instead of outside the Limestone mine for security purposes, because it's fortified and easier to secure, and we don't have to take everyone in and out through security each time."

Adrianna leaned in toward Greg. "Do you have many security threats at the Vault?"

Laughing, Greg shook his head. "Nope. I mean, yes, there is a lot of secure information in the Vault and a few very rich individuals keep their personal collections of valuables down there, but it's one of the most secure places in the States that isn't owned by the military. No one has tried to break in, and I don't think anyone is going to anytime soon."

Adrianna ate her last French fry. "Have you been in that locked room we walked to for the fire drill? Do you know what it looks like inside?"

Beverly stopped by, picked up their empty dinner plates, and sat a fresh piece of bright red cherry pie in front of both of them. Greg picked up his fork, but kept talking. "Yes, actually, part of the security team's job is to make sure that they stock the Vault with up-to-date materials. Roughly a year ago, I had to help take some expired foods out and restocked it. Honestly, we didn't do too much, though, because most of what they have in there are things like MREs that last between ten to thirty years before needing to be replaced."

He took a bite of pie and then continued to talk. "Behind the door you saw, there are actually multiple rooms. There's one room that's like a storeroom with shelves upon shelves of dry goods. Another room is hooked into our plumbing system, with multiple bathroom stalls and showers, and then four small rooms with cots and blankets that could be set up in the case of an emergency. There's also one more door, but even I wasn't allowed inside that one. The rumor is that it's for some type of VIP to escape to in the case of an emergency. Probably some big political figures, maybe even the president himself. All I know is that the area is the most secure place in the entire facility."

Their dinner may have been nothing special, but this pie was out of this world. Each bite of cherry burst in her mouth, and the crust was the perfect amount of sweet and flakey. Adrianna took a sip of her water. "This pie is out of this world. I might need to get some to-go. Is there really a lake down in the Vault too?"

His eyebrow raised. "Wow, the rumor mill really goes around quickly, doesn't it? To answer your question, yes, there is a large reservoir down there, although it's not rated for drinking. We have a filtration system that takes that water and cleans it for consumption, but they also use it for all the sink and bathroom needs in this place. It does eventually go out into the public sewage system, and the reservoir refills naturally from an underground river.

He gave her a half smile. "It's the exact location, though, I'm not allowed to divulge. That area is totally off limits for employees because they don't want anyone messing with the water supply down there."

They finished up the rest of their dessert and talked a bit about working at the Vault. Adrianna was so glad they had extended their time past coffee. This was much better than the place right beside the sports stadium. She wasn't distracted by Charles's drama outside her window here. Despite the scrutiny of the locals, she was having a really delightful time. The more she learned about Greg, the more she couldn't shake the fact that she'd never met a man as genuine as him before, and probably never would again.

People came over periodically through their meal to say a quick hello to Greg and to look her over. They peppered her with lots of questions that made her feel self-conscious, but after seeing her squirm, Greg soon jumped in and started directing the conversations away from her.

The only one that couldn't be redirected was an older woman named Beatrice. She seemed like she was trying to conduct a background investigation right there in the diner. They were sure protective of their part-time police officer.

They were finishing up their last few bites when Greg got a phone call. He answered it right there at the table, nodded his head, and put down his napkin over the top of the last remnants of his pie. "I have to go. I got a call about some teenagers at the Arcadianville lookout. It's a common make-out spot for the young locals. I can either drop you off at home, or you could come and help me chase off a couple of hooligans. Which would you prefer?"

Not wanting to leave her cheery company and go back to an empty house, Adrianna decided to spend a bit more time with the real man, Greg, instead of the plant she'd named after him. She placed her own napkin over an empty plate similar to Greg. "Sure, I'd love to come. I make great hooligan-scaring backup."

Chapter Seventeen: The Case of the Hooligans

*A*drianna

Driving slowly through the winding roads, they made their way to the lookout point. Greg seemed a little quieter than before, but Adrianna didn't know if it was because he was being extra cautious of the roads at night, or if he'd moved into work mode.

They pulled up behind a car that was sitting in front of them with all the windows fogged up. It shook slightly from side to side. Greg leaned over to her before opening his door. "Stay here. I have a feeling I'm about to get more of an eyeful than I want to see. I should be back in just a minute."

Adrianna stayed in the car as she watched Greg go up to the driver's side of the car and knock on the window. He held his badge up to the edge of the window. As Adrianna watched, she couldn't help but smirk with amusement, but her eyebrows shot up as she saw the passenger door fling open. She saw a teenage boy dart out of the car shirtless, trying to buckle his pants while running.

She saw Greg throw up his arms and yell something after the boy. Then he pulled out a flashlight and ran into the woods after him. It looked like they were going to be here longer than they originally thought. Adrianna got out of the car and turned the flashlight on her phone to see if anyone else in the car needed help.

Walking up to the driver's door, it surprised her to find that the person inside was an older woman. The woman was probably in her mid-sixties, wearing an elegant skirt and blouse and a tasteful white jacket over it. The woman put her window down as she saw Adrianna approaching.

Taken aback, Adrianna cautiously approached. "Ma'am, is everything alright?"

The woman arranged her blouse. "I'm so terribly embarrassed. This was just a fling. I've been so lonely since my husband passed three years ago. I guess I just got caught up in the flattery of a twenty-two-year-old trying to woo me. Jacob didn't want his roommates to know about us, and I didn't want my nosy neighbors seeing him come to my house, so we came here. I thought we would be all alone."

It seemed like Greg had just as many interesting stories as she did. Although, he actually was part of them in real life, while she just read about them.

Greg walked up with the young man who was hugging his bare chest, following close behind with his head hung low. "I checked your friend's license, and you two are free to go with only a warning, but I suggest finding another location to meet up next time."

The old woman thanked Greg and quickly drove off with her young lover.

Greg chuckled before turning to Adrianna. "So much for just grabbing coffee. Sorry to drag you all over the countryside tonight."

Adrianna smiled. "I wouldn't have missed it. Besides, you obviously needed the backup. What would you have done if the woman had run in the opposite direction?"

Greg chuckled as he held the door open for Adrianna. "I guess I would have had to run them both down. I could have called another local police officer if I needed backup, but it looked like I could handle those two." This was one non-date that she would always remember.

Greg came in and sat down in the car beside her, but turned to her to talk before starting up his truck. "See, that was easy enough. I know most of my calls around here are superficial, but sometimes I also get called when someone has a chainsaw accident or falls from a ladder. I like my job here." He sat for a moment quietly, looking out over the dark gorge. "You know, you should really come up here with me during the daylight sometime. The view really is magnificent."

Did that mean that he was suggesting a real date? Her heart fluttered at the thought. She really wanted to see him again. Adrianna shrugged and tried to reply nonchalantly, "Sure, I'd love that."

"Great, then I will check my work schedule and we'll set something up." He smiled from ear to ear. It seemed Greg was a man of action, not one to just throw out thoughts and not follow up on them.

She watched him out of the corner of her eye as she asked him, "Did you ever bring girls up here when you were a teenager?"

He laughed out loud. "Yes, actually, I used to in high school, or at least I did before the accident."

"Accident? What exactly happened?" *Is he referring to what happened to his face?*

"It happened my senior year of high school. I'll have you know that in my younger days, I was quite the woman-chaser. Although, that guy didn't understand that more lies below the surface of a woman than just her looks. Anyway, it was a few days before the big homecoming game, and I was speeding along these back country roads feeling like I was invincible and nothing bad could ever happen to me. Of course, I didn't have my seatbelt on. A drunk driver came out of nowhere and hit the front of my car. I went through the windshield." He pointed to his face and angled himself close for her to examine his scar. "As you can see, I will never forget that accident. That's actually when I decided I wanted to help keep people safe. If that man hadn't been drunk driving, he wouldn't have lost his life, and his little girl would still have a dad. If I had been driving slower, I would have been able to stop before he hit me, and if I was wearing a seatbelt, I wouldn't have ruined my face. I now stick to the letter of the law because it's there for a reason."

He sat silently for a few moments, as if waiting to see how Adrianna would respond. The moment felt so intimate that Adrianna lifted her finger and, as gently as she could, ran it over the top of the scarred skin. He shivered under her touch, but didn't jerk away. As if spellbound by her touch, he sat silently as she gently traced the white curves across his cheekbone and down to his slightly stubbly chin.

Very softly, Adrianna said, "You didn't ruin your face. You know, I don't really even notice it anymore, now that I'm getting to know you. Does it hurt?"

He took her hand from his face, engulfing it in his own. "It used to hurt a lot, especially when I smiled. I went through a few very dark years right after the accident until finally I decided that wasn't how I wanted to live my life. It took a lot of willpower to accept that I should be grateful for any life I have to live and for not dying in that accident. I had to force myself to smile at first, but eventually the scar tissue got used to the movement and now it barely hurts at all."

He let her hand go and cleared his throat, breaking the intimate feel of the occasion. He started up the car and backed up. "I'm sorry I talked about myself so much tonight, but I appreciate you having a friendly, open ear to listen. I had a nice evening with you. Sometimes it just feels great to be with a friend that things click with. If you want to try this again, I promise I will do more listening. You mentioned you didn't know what to do with the plants outside your quaint little cottage. I have off Saturday morning. Do you want me to swing by and teach you how to care for them? "

She smiled. "Sure, I'll make French toast for breakfast... if you want?"

"Can't wait!" He dropped her off in front of her cottage, waiting in the driveway until she was safely inside.

Adrianna locked the door and leaned against it. She looked over at her plant. One leaf was turning yellow. "Greg, I just had a wonderful night with your namesake. He seems pretty adamant about the friend thing, but do you think he might be interested in something more once we get to know each other better?" Moving closer to examine the plant, Adrianna set down her keys and purse on the counter. "He is going to teach me about plants, so I can't let you die. Are you thirsty again? Maybe I should give you some more water." Adrianna took a cup from the sink and poured it over the plant, oblivious to the water pooling around its base.

Chapter Eighteen: The Case of the Alzheimer's Patient

G^{reg}

Greg drove home humming to himself. He had a pleasant time with Adrianna, but such a hard time reading her. He was used to women who flirted and talked nonstop. Adrianna talked, but barely said a hundred words all night. Instead, she kept encouraging him to talk about himself.

As for flirting, he looked for the normal signs of women touching his shoulder or sitting close to him, but he didn't see Adrianna do any of that. He was really feeling like he had a one-sided crush until that moment in the car. She hadn't touched him at all until he started opening up about himself and the accident. Most of the locals knew his story, so he wasn't expecting to see the compassion in her eyes as she gently lifted her hand. Subconsciously, he had leaned into her gentle, curious fingers. No one had touched him that intimately since his accident.

Her simple words rolled over in his mind repeatedly. *You didn't ruin your face. I don't even notice it anymore.* Was it possible she saw beyond the scars to the man beneath?

Greg wasn't sure what it meant, but he felt a strange sense of hope as he drove home. He was still unsure if Adrianna was actually interested in him, but he knew one thing for sure. He was definitely interested in her.

Walking up to his dark house, it suddenly felt empty, like it never had before. He quickly showered, pulled on some boxers, and hopped into bed. His shift at the Vault started early tomorrow. He hadn't planned on staying out so late, shooing away lovers and talking with Adrianna, and now he only had a few hours to sleep before he needed to get ready for his next shift.

In a way, he was being truthful when he said he was too busy with work to date, even if he used it as an excuse to avoid rejection. After tonight, he didn't know what to think. Maybe he should have just stayed quiet and waited patiently to see what she would've said to Henrietta's set-up.

He laid his head upon his pillow, trying to clear his mind and failing. All he could think about was Adrianna. Suddenly, his phone started ringing, and Greg groaned as he rolled over and answered without even looking at the number. At this time of night, he could guess who was calling.

"Hello?"

He was right; it was the police secretary. "I'm so sorry to call you again tonight, especially so late, but I need you to help find Tom Wilson. His son says he can't find him anywhere, and he's worried because the man is in his nineties and has Alzheimer's."

Greg groaned as he sat up. "I'll head right over. Text me the address." He may have mourned his lost slumber, but prayed Tom was safe.

He knew all too well that another sleepless night was ahead. He ached to be with Adrianna and to feel the warmth of her presence, but the burden of saving this town's crises weighed too heavily on him to try a genuine relationship. No matter how much he liked Adrianna, what relationship could survive him running out during dates and in the middle of the night? Even after he came home, he would always have to keep everything he did confidential. When they next met, he needed to stick to his gut that he only had time for a casual friendship, no matter how strong his feelings ran.

Greg grabbed a blanket for the missing man and steeled himself against the darkness as he drove off into the night. He was determined to reach Tom before the man got himself into serious trouble.

The night was a blur of speed walking through the local forest, calling for the man. He was just thinking about calling in a full manhunt when he found Tom sitting on a log watching the stars.

"Tom! There you are. Are you alright?"

The old man looked over at him and whispered, "You know, my wife loves to look at the stars. We sit here and watch them all the time, you know?"

Knowing that his wife had passed a few years back, Greg was glad the darkness hid the pity in his eyes. "Tom, I don't think your wife is coming tonight. Why don't you come home with me? Your son is really worried."

Greg wrapped him in the warm blanket he'd brought, called his son, and radioed the station to alert them that Tom was alright. Slowly, he led the man along the trails with only a flashlight to guide them. Tom's son thanked him for his help, and Greg looked at his clock. His shift as a security guard was going to begin in less than an hour, not leaving him enough time to go home and get a good amount of sleep. He stopped home to change into his uniform before driving by the local diner. He sleepily greeted his sister, who was baking bread, pies, and donuts for when she officially opened for the day.

"Look at you, up before the sunshine. What has you here this early?" Beverly asked. She grabbed a mug and poured him a cup of coffee. "Did you spend the night working, or were you with that woman I saw you with earlier this evening?"

Greg gave a half-smile as he briefly imagined what his evening would have been like if he'd spent it with Adrianna. Even if nothing had happened between them, that was where he would have preferred to spend his time. He was always happy to be busy and lending a hand all around town. It was only recently that he felt so possessive of his time. He tried to shrug it off. He was probably grumpy from the lack of sleep this evening.

"I was up all night with police work. I know I'm only working part-time there, but it seems like this town can be very needy sometimes. Don't get that suspicious look on your face about Adrianna. She is just a new employee at the Vault, and I was showing her around. Don't worry, there is nothing there but a friendship. I don't have time for anything else, even if she was interested."

Beverly raised an eyebrow and shook her head. "Uh-huh. You were just being friendly last night as you leaned toward her every word and barely took your eyes off her. I'm sure that was all that was going on."

Greg grunted his reply and poured himself a second much-needed cup of coffee to-go. Greg drove to his second job at the Vault, trying to keep himself awake. He was glad that he was helpful last night, but he was just too exhausted today.

He replayed the events of last night and could not shake his emotions from being tied to the pretty girl that was Adrianna. Not too long after his shift started, he saw her walk into the guardhouse and place her bags on the X-ray's conveyor belt as she checked in. Suddenly, he didn't feel sleepy or grumpy at all. She gave him a bright smile in greeting, and everything felt right in his world.

Chapter Nineteen: The Case of the Unsuspecting Napper

G *reg*

Greg's eyelids cracked open when the light hit them. Today was thankfully the weekend. While he still had a few hours of police work to do this evening, at least he didn't have to do a shift at the Vault today. He laid in bed for a few minutes, enjoying the feeling of rest, until a stray thought of Adrianna flitted through his mind. The sun was glowing, and Greg had promised to help Adrianna with the flowers outside her home. It was a good excuse to see her. She said she wasn't much of a gardener, and he wanted to make sure they looked their best for her.

With a groan he got out of bed, and within a few minutes he was hopping into his truck. He pulled up to her quaint cottage, and as he grabbed his gardening tools out of the back of his truck, he noticed Adrianna sitting on a swing, reading a book outside of her cottage. The sight stirred his heartstrings, and his eyes weren't focused on the flowers. Greg held up a hand shovel. "Good morning! I was hoping you still wanted to learn a little about gardening this morning. Is this a good time?"

"Hi, Greg! Yes, I was just enjoying a good book. Thank you so much for coming over to help me," Adrianna greeted him with a warm smile.

"No problem," Greg replied. A yawn tried to escape, and he rubbed the sleep out of his eyes. "Sorry about that. I'm still just a little tired after I pulled an all-nighter between my jobs yesterday."

Adrianna's brow furrowed with concern. "Are you sure you're up for this? I promised you French toast. We can just go inside and have a late breakfast if you want?"

"No, I'll be fine," Greg assured her, returning her smile. "Let's get to work. I just need to get my blood pumping."

Greg showed Adrianna how to trim the dead leaves off the flowers and water them properly. She watched him with great interest as he worked his magic. He was so focused on the task at hand that he forgot how exhausted he was.

"Ouch!" Adrianna yelped as a small prickle of blood escaped a rose thorn wound on her pointer finger.

Before he could think about it, Greg leaned over and kissed the back of her hand. "You might want to put a band-aid on that so you don't get dirt in it." Adrianna stood stock still, staring at her finger for a moment, and Greg was kicking himself for overstepping their friendship boundary. Another yawn tried to escape, but he did his best to stifle it. He didn't want her to think he was bored.

"Hey, you look like you could use a break, and I need to fetch a band-aid," Adrianna said with a gentle smile. "Come on in and have a seat on the couch. I'll make us some lemonade and something to eat."

Greg hesitated for a moment, glancing at the flowers that still needed tending outside. "Are you sure? I'm supposed to be teaching you how to take care of these, and we barely got to half," he said, gesturing to the flowerbeds.

Adrianna chuckled. "Don't worry about it. We can tackle those later. Right now, I think you need to take a load off and cool down."

With a nod, Greg followed her inside and took a seat on the couch. Adrianna bustled off toward the kitchen while he leaned back, closing his eyes and taking a deep breath. The coolness of the air-conditioning felt like heaven against his overheated skin.

When Greg finally woke up, he looked around, confused. There was a blanket laid across him, dirt and all, and the glass of lemonade sitting beside him had ice cubes that were almost all melted. "What happened?"

"You fell asleep on my couch," Adrianna said with a smile. She was sitting in a rocking chair across the room from him, curled up with her legs underneath her, reading a book. From the half-naked man on the front, he assumed it must be some kind of steamy romance.

Greg rubbed his eyes and stood up. "I'm so sorry. I didn't mean to fall asleep."

Adrianna laughed. "It's okay. You looked so peaceful. Did you get some rest?"

Greg nodded and looked at the time on his phone. "Yeah, I feel a lot better. I should probably head out, though. I have to get some sleep before my next shift at the police station."

"Of course," Adrianna said. She seemed understanding, but the tone of her voice dipped in a way that Greg wondered if she was as disappointed as he was that he had to leave already. "Thank you for coming over and helping me with the flowers. The first half looks beautiful now, and I'm sure I can handle the other half."

Greg smiled. "I'm glad I could help. And hey, maybe next time we can do something that doesn't involve me falling asleep on your couch."

Adrianna laughed. "That would be nice. Have a good rest, Greg."

"You too, Adrianna." Greg gave her a small wave as he walked out the door.

Greg climbed into his truck, feeling a mix of disappointment and gratitude. Disappointed that he had to leave Adrianna so soon, but grateful for the brief rest and her understanding. He started the engine and pulled away from her cottage, making a mental note to plan something more enjoyable for their next meeting.

That evening, Greg found himself back at the police station for a few hours, trying to focus on the tasks at hand. His thoughts kept returning to Adrianna, her bright smile, and the way she had gazed at him. He knew he wanted to see her again soon, and that scared him. He tried to shake her from his head. She was so far out of his league that he knew he should try to keep his distance instead of looking forward to seeing her again.

He sat at his desk, going through paperwork. His shift was almost over, and he didn't have any calls tonight, so it was a good time to get caught up on the never-ending onslaught of forms. His phone buzzed with a call. Glancing at the screen, he saw it was from Adrianna. He quickly answered it.

"Greg, I need your help!" Adrianna's voice was frantic, her breathing heavy. "There's a bear in my garden, and it chased me up a tree! I don't know what to do!"

Greg's heart skipped a beat. "Stay calm, Adrianna. I'll be there as soon as I can. Just stay in the tree and don't make any sudden movements."

He rushed to his truck and sped off toward Adrianna's cottage. As he pulled up, he could see the destruction the bear had caused. The once-beautiful flower garden was now a mess of upturned soil, crushed plants, and scattered petals. And there, high in a tree, was Adrianna, clinging to a branch, looking terrified.

Adrianna's eyes widened with relief when she saw him. "Thank goodness you're here, Greg!"

Greg quickly scanned the area but saw no sign of the bear. "I think the bear is gone for now, but we need to get you down from there. Just take it slow and be careful."

He guided her down from the tree, and once she was safely on the ground, they both let out a sigh of relief.

"Are you okay?" Greg asked, concern clear in his voice.

Adrianna nodded, still shaken. "Yeah, I'm okay. Thank you so much for coming to help me."

"We'll call animal control, and they'll handle it from here. In the meantime, let's see if we can salvage anything from your garden."

Together, they assessed the damage and began picking up the scattered flowers, trying to save whatever they could. "Make sure you call your landlord and let him know about the damages. Despite our hard work, it's going to take a while to grow back in." As they worked, they talked about their day, their laughter filling the air despite the unfortunate situation.

As they stood in the fading sunlight, Greg couldn't help but give Adrianna some advice about dealing with black bears. "Adrianna, I just wanted to mention that it's not really safe to climb a tree when you see a black bear. They're actually excellent climbers, and you could have been putting yourself in more danger."

Adrianna looked at him with surprise. "Really? I didn't know that. What should I have done instead?"

"Well, you should try to make a lot of noise and make yourself look big. You can do this by waving your arms, shouting, and standing on your tiptoes. Black bears are usually more scared of us than we are of them, so making yourself seem like a threat can often scare them away," Greg explained.

Adrianna nodded, taking in the information. "Thank you for telling me, Greg. I'll definitely remember that next time. I hope there won't be a next time, though."

Greg smiled. "I hope so too. But just in case, it's always good to be prepared." They stood silently for a few moments, looking over the garden.

"I really appreciate your help, Greg," Adrianna said, wiping the sweat from her brow. "I don't know what I would have done without you."

Greg smiled. "It's no problem at all. Just let me know if you need anything else. And maybe next time, we can plan something a little more fun."

Adrianna laughed. "Yeah, I'd like that. No bears or falling asleep on couches."

Chapter Twenty: The Case of the Closed Investigation

A^{drianna}

Adrianna's mind kept straying back to her fun night with Greg. She probably shouldn't have touched his cheek. It was an uncharacteristically bold move on her part that was spurred by the intimate moment, but she feared she had pushed him too far, too fast.

He made it clear that he only wanted to be friends and seemed nervous and drove her home shortly after she touched him. She would keep her feelings to herself and keep things purely platonic, so she didn't ruin their burgeoning friendship. Right now, she needed all the friends she could get.

Frowning, Adrianna double-checked the case she was working on sitting in front of her. They'd marked it as closed, but there was no report written up reviewing the case. Was she reading this right? She took it to Henrietta.

"Hey, can you look at this case for me? It says closed, but I haven't reviewed it yet, and I looked it up in the system. No one else reviewed it either. If I'm reading this right, he is getting awarded his clearance without his background check being completed."

Henrietta took the case from Adrianna's hands. "Here, let me look."

She zoomed through a few pages and furrowed her brow. "Do you see here, it was due yesterday and marked complete yesterday, but you're right. They interviewed this individual, but they never fully reviewed his case. This was probably just a simple clerical error somewhere along the line, but the government takes this kind of potential security threat seriously. You should take this to Darren to make sure he's aware of it."

Adrianna took back the case file, and Henrietta went back to work. She walked up to Darren's office and knocked on his opened door. He looked up from his computer and gave her a slimy smile that put her on edge. "Come on in. What can I do for you, Adrianna?"

Placing the case file in front of him, Adrianna pointed to the case number. "I found this case that seems to be closed prematurely, and Henrietta suggested I bring it to you."

The smile fell away from Darren's face. "It's good you brought this to me. We need to ensure that we do everything correctly and take these security clearances seriously. Who else did you tell about this?"

Adrianna shrugged. "I just showed Henrietta because I wasn't sure if I was missing something."

"Good, good. Next time you can just bring these to me. You can leave this one here, and I'll figure out what happened and take care of making sure it gets thoroughly reviewed."

Adrianna nodded and backed away from the office. As soon as she was out of Darren's sight, she blew out the breath she hadn't realized she was holding. She did not know why that man rubbed her the wrong way, but she always got a bad feeling when she was around him.

Although she was glad to find a potential problem before it became a bigger one; she was quickly learning that being a background investigator had its responsibilities, and it was up to her to make sure they did the job right.

Relieved that she could put the case in the right hands, Adrianna headed back to her desk. Luckily, Darren seemed more concerned with the investigation being done properly than assigning blame. She would have to remember to keep her eye out for errors like this from now on and bring it directly to her boss if it were to happen again.

Their department's workload was backing up, so Adrianna dived back into her work, not giving the closed case another thought. It was a bit past her normal lunchtime when she finished up the case she was reviewing and realized how hungry she was.

Grabbing her sandwich to-go, Adrianna took a bite as she rushed out of her secure room and into the cave's corridors. She looked forward to her daily walk and the chance to see the sunshine and one specific smiling face. Greg.

To her shock, he was standing right outside her door. He gave her his bright smile that seemed to light up the dank tunnels. "Adrianna! I was hoping you would come out for your walk around this time like you normally do."

Adrianna tried to reply, but ended up mumbling as she tried to cover her mouth, that was full of a bite of sandwich. She swallowed and tried again. "Greg, so nice to see you. What brings you to my door?" She had as much romantic game as a cricket. No wonder he just wanted to be friends.

"You expressed an interest in this cave system, and I was wondering if you wanted me to show you around the public pathways? There isn't a lot to see, and there are some areas that are off limits to you, but there is still a lot of ground to cover. If you're interested."

"That is so sweet! I would love to. Do you mind if I finish my sandwich while we walk? I only have a half-hour lunch before I have to get back to all the work piling up on my desk." For some reason, she no longer cared about whether she would see the sun. Apparently, that was never really her destination, just her excuse.

"Sure, whatever you want."

They walked down a corridor Adrianna had never used before. The way these tunnels twisted and passed over each other was like a maze that would take forever to walk, and they could only explore for fifteen minutes before returning from her half-hour lunch. She didn't mind Greg's offer, but it surprised her. He genuinely seemed to like her, but he was definitely shying away from anything more. Did he have something he wanted to talk about with a friend or just wanted to spend time with her like someone interested in more?

She wasn't great at subtle conversation, so Adrianna got right to the point. "So, what made you decide to seek me out today? Did you have something you wanted to talk about?"

He shook his head. "Not particularly, just wanted to show you around. None of my other friends or family have clearance to be down here, so I thought I would help you take full advantage of yours."

They walked to an enormous cavern that was currently being dug out with large machines and trucks. Greg stopped and watched them for a bit. "This corridor is where most of the current expansion is going on. They recently ran electricity a few hundred yards more in this direction and are currently adding a dozen more large secure rooms, similar to the one you work in. I don't know what companies or parts of the government will operate out of them, but I thought it was kind of neat seeing them in the process of being built."

They watched a truck full of dirt drive past them. "Do those guys have clearance?"

"As I'm sure you know, there are different levels of clearance. I have to have a high one because I have access to this entire facility, and I'm sure that you have a high one to be allowed to process other people's background checks. These guys have a more basic background check completed since they don't have access to anywhere that holds sensitive information, but everyone, including the guy who refills your water cooler, has to have one to be down here."

Adrianna looked at her watch, disappointed that their short time was almost over. "I have to head back. Thank you for showing me this. I have to admit, it's intimidating to explore these tunnels alone, and it's a lot more fun to get some exercise with a friend."

They started walking back to Adrianna's room. Adrianna had to pick up the pace to get back on time, but Greg's long legs seemed to have no trouble keeping up. "I'm glad you could come. Same time tomorrow?"

Her lunch breaks just got a lot more interesting. "I look forward to it."

He nodded his head. "Great, I'm not allowed to take you to the underground lake, but I'll take you to see the next best thing."

Chapter Twenty-One:
The Case of the Lone Bike Ride

A *drianna*

The sun shone through the trees, casting a crisp light on the surrounding forest. Adrianna pedaled her borrowed bike along the gravel path, feeling the breeze ruffle her hair and the warmth of the sun on her skin.

She had moved out to the middle of nowhere only a few months ago, and she was glad that she had done so. The slower pace of life was something she was coming to appreciate. It fit her independent lifestyle.

Adrianna felt the wind as she glided down a hill on a bike she'd rented at Greg's suggestion. He was good at getting her out of her comfort zone and encouraging her to do something different from staying at home reading a romance novel. He apologized for missing their bike ride today, but some kind of security emergency popped up at the Limestone Vault. After the third time he insisted she go without him, she agreed so that he would stop apologizing for having to cancel on her.

Home. Her cottage and this backcountry place were starting to feel like she belonged here.

The bike path wound its way through the woods beside a babbling stream, and then into a pitch-black tunnel. As the light grew dimmer, she slowed down, barely making anything out but the crunching of the gravel beneath her tires as she pedaled. She knew this path was an old train track that was converted to a bike trail, but it was still unnerving.

When she could no longer see any light, she thought she heard a soft scraping sound. A shiver ran down her spine as she tried to decide if she should stop or peddle faster. She continued to go slowly as she tentatively yelled out, "Hello?"

Immediately, she heard a man's deep voice reply, "Sorry, I didn't realize anyone was in here. I'm close to the edge of the tunnel. I'll back out so we don't accidentally run into one another."

Peddling cautiously, after what felt like an eternity, she emerged into the light. It took a moment for her eyes to adjust, but when she did, she couldn't help but stop dead and stare. It was Charles. One of the first cases she'd reviewed, the Romeo to Dana's Juliette, the man she saw getting yelled at outside of a Bumblebees game.

She stared dumbly, and he gave her a bright smile. "Glad you made it through! My name's Charles. How is your ride going?"

Adrianna realized that the details of his case were getting fuzzy in her head now that she had reviewed so many people's backgrounds. She recognized his face and remembered he liked karaoke and sports, but that was about it. Apparently, he liked to go biking too. It was a lot easier to meet someone when you didn't know their entire life history beforehand.

After taking a drink from her water bottle to distract from her awkwardness, Adrianna held out a hand for Charles to shake. She would do better than her first meeting with Dana; that had made her want to hide in shame. It was just eerie seeing someone on paper almost come to life. "Yes, it's a beautiful day. Didn't want to stay home all cooped up. My name is Adrianna. Nice to meet you."

"Can't agree more! Well, I better get moving if I want to get in ten more miles today. It was nice to meet you, Adrianna. Maybe I'll see you again," the man replied, with a hint of a smile curling his lips. His eyes slowly looked her over. He jumped on his bike and took off into the tunnel.

She hopped on her bike and kept going, while her mind swirled with possibilities. A part of her really wished there weren't pesky privacy laws, and that she was the kind of person who could bend the rules sometimes. Now that she'd met both Dana and Charles in person, she was more convinced than ever that they should meet. They were both good-looking individuals that had similar interests and mannerisms. She knew if she could just get them in the same room together, sparks would fly.

She bit her lip. She couldn't bring herself to break someone's confidentiality and meddle in the lives of others. A matchmaker she was not. Instead of being in everyone's business, she was the one who sat on the sidelines and watched the drama of other people's lives objectively, and she wanted to keep it that way.

Adrianna ate the lunch she packed herself beside a gurgling stream, before riding back and returning the bike. It was such a pleasant afternoon, but she was tired from all the exercise and couldn't wait to get back to the romance novel she was reading, *Falling for the Scotsman*. She was getting to the good part where the Laird was going to profess his love somewhere romantic.

Feeling a twinge of sadness, Adrianna couldn't help but think of Greg. While she had a little silly crush on the charismatic officer, they were friends and nothing more. Sometimes it was more fun to read a silly romance novel than people's backgrounds because you could count on there always being that happy ending.

I'm too much of an awkward introvert to get that kind of fairytale ending. I need to stay content with the way things are.

As Adrianna drove home, she kept thinking of Charles and Dana. She may not be able to make anyone fall in love, but she could work on being more content with her own current love life. This bike trip was a good beginning. She didn't want to wait for Greg when he clearly wasn't interested. Maybe it was good Greg didn't join her, so she could take some time to work on herself right now.

Adrianna got into her car and spent the rest of her drive home brainstorming ways to feel more content with things the way they were. By the way she talked to her plant like a roommate, it was apparent that she needed some relationships in her life. Instead of worrying about her lack of a love life with Greg, she would work on her friendships with Henrietta and Greg.

Head held high with the endorphins of a good workout coursing through her system, she decided to start taking charge of her social life right then and there. Now it was time for action, with the part of her life she struggled with most. People. With renewed energy, Adrianna called Greg's phone to see if he was free to hang out as friends after he was done with his shift.

A woman's voice answered, and Adrianna couldn't catch her heart as it sank. "Hello?"

Chapter Twenty-Two: The Case of the Big Fire

G^{reg} During their lunchtime walk, Greg couldn't help himself from continually glancing over at Adrianna. She was beautiful and quirky in her own way. He had to admit; he was smitten.

A battle raged inside him since their time at the lookout when they weren't on a date. No matter what excuses he kept coming up with, he finally decided he liked her too much to just stay friends. No matter how busy he was or how important his job was, he needed Adrianna in his life.

He planned to ask her out on a proper date when they went bike riding together, but then he got called into work. It seemed minor security issues kept popping up a lot lately. He could help get everything squared away fairly quickly, but not soon enough for his time with Adrianna.

Greg fiddled with one of the buttons on his uniform as they walked. "So, Adrianna. How is your morning going?"

"There is a pile of papers on my desk a mile high, but otherwise, it's going well. I've definitely had a few interesting cases to keep me on my toes for sure. Your sister seems very nice. Just out of curiosity, do you spend a lot of time with her?"

Adrianna picked up her pace as natural sunlight came into view, and Greg easily matched her stride. His sister must have left quite an impression that time they saw her at the diner a few weeks ago. "I see her regularly, simply because we both live in the same small town, but I don't see her every day. Yesterday evening, my sister needed someone to watch Andrew and Gabby when she was called into work at the last minute. I ended up having a late lunch with the three of them before she took off for work."

Looking at him from the corner of her eye, Adrianna said. "So I heard. I tried to call you, but your sister Beverly answered. She had quite a few questions for me."

Greg groaned. He would have to talk with Bev. She had his best interests at heart, but sometimes she could be a bit too overbearing when it came to his personal life. "Oh, I'm sorry. She should mind her own business. I'm sorry I missed your call."

They walked toward the Vault's entrance, and he watched as Adrianna stopped short when the sunshine hit her. She closed her eyes and lifted her head to soak in the rays. As he watched her, he could feel his heart racing as he took a deep breath and steeled himself to make the move. He had to be brave and risk it all if he wanted something more to come from his friendship with Adrianna.

She seemed receptive. She said she didn't notice his scars anymore, but the truth was he still couldn't shake the feeling that he wasn't good enough because of his looks. For a man with nerves of steel when facing rabid animals and drunk hunters, he was having the hardest time bringing himself to ask her out on a date. Her rejection scared him more than anything else in his life ever had. "So, Adrianna…"

Adrianna opened her eyes and looked at him expectantly. Her lips partially parted, a few strands of her hair shimmered in the sunlight. "Yes?"

He lost his nerve. "Oh, it's just getting close to the time we should get you back to your room."

They started walking back down the dark tunnels, their eyes adjusting to the dimmer lighting. Maybe he should try something easier and invite her to a local bonfire party one of his friends was hosting? Couples paired off and took walks in the woods together all the time. Maybe he would be braver in the moonlight, where his scars weren't as obvious.

They were almost back to Adrianna's room when she looked over at him with her large doe-like eyes. "Is something bothering you, Greg? You are usually a lot more talkative than today."

He couldn't tell her about his insecurities over his looks, so he spouted off the first excuse that came to mind. "Yeah, I'm fine, just kicking myself for making you go bike riding without me. While it needed to be investigated, that security issue I was telling you about ended up being a minor error in the system. We double-checked everything multiple times, and it appeared everything was working fine. I feel like I just wasted a perfectly good morning. I would have preferred to spend it with you."

They stopped in front of the door, out of the way of anyone coming and going. Adrianna glanced down at her watch. "Well, if that's all that's bothering you, we can just plan to go again."

A stray hair had escaped Adrianna's ponytail during their walk. Before he could stop himself, he reached up and gently tucked it behind her ear. "Actually, I was wondering if you were free to go to a bonfire with me? My friend Jimmy is throwing a bonfire party on Friday. He does this once or twice a summer, and he always has lots of snacks. It's a fun time."

Adrianna looked at her watch again and dread formed in Greg's chest. *She must not want to go. Did she not want to go with him? Was she mad he ditched her the other day for work? Did she have plans with someone else who wasn't afraid to ask her out?*

The moment stretched as he waited for her response, feeling like his entire world was hanging on her answer. A slow smile grew across her lips, and she said, "Yes, that sounds nice. I'd love to go, but I need to head back to my desk. My lunch break is over."

"Sounds good. I'll text you the details."

Greg watched as Adrianna gave him a parting smile, swiped her badge, and entered her office. He felt an initial burst of excitement because the bonfire seemed like the perfect place to find the courage to ask her if she wanted to be more than friends.

Then his mind started running through potential scenarios and conversations in his head. *They would enjoy themselves at the bonfire when Greg would nonchalantly ask her if she wanted to take a little stroll down a nearby well-cared-for path. They would walk close together and stop somewhere private under the pretense of looking for an owl. She would be chilly and snuggle close enough to him that he could put his arm around her in order to keep her warm. She would tilt her head up to thank him, and he would lower his lips to meet hers...*

Greg's fantasy stopped as he tried to figure out what Adrianna would do. Would she let him kiss her? Would she turn her head, trying to hide her revulsion? Maybe she would start walking quickly back to the campfire, so they weren't alone anymore.

Whatever happened, he had a feeling that he would torture himself with these potential scenarios until Friday night actually occurred. He felt a weight in the pit of his stomach and knew that he couldn't keep this up. He needed to tell her how he felt on Friday night, no matter how it ended.

He ran through a few more scenarios where he asked her permission before kissing her or told her how she lit up his day. Sometimes his mind let him imagine what it would feel like to press her soft lips against his own, but most of the time he felt the harsh rejection that he feared. It really would be easier and safer to remain friends, but he couldn't keep up the pretense any longer. Even the thought of her was driving him crazy because he was falling for her.

Chapter Twenty-Three:
The Case of the
Soon-to-Be
Employee

*A*drianna

The fire burned fiercely, its flames and smoke reaching high into the sky. Adrianna stood on the outskirts of the group as people around it talked and laughed, hanging around it like moths drawn to its center. The firelight played on their faces and lips, painting them orange.

It was very nice of Greg to invite her to come, but honestly, it was pretty overwhelming. She had jumped at the chance to spend more time with Greg, but now that she was here, she couldn't let her guard down. Greg was talking and laughing with a few people on his way to get them both some pizza, but all she could see were the half-formed faces and shadows of strangers in the darkness.

Upon further inspection, it looked like he was talking to none other than Dana Hemsworth. They both looked her way, and she gave a small wave. She hoped she could hold a conversation with the woman without being so awkward like last time.

Greg walked over and handed her a drink and a plate of pizza. "You don't have to hide over here. I know the fire is hot, but I almost couldn't find you."

Adrianna took her drink and plate from him. "I was taking a few minutes to take in my surroundings. Thank you for the food. I'm starved. Do you mind if we take our food for a walk? It seems like there is a nice open path over there, and I saw a few other people go that way."

Greg didn't respond right away, so Adrianna continued, "I mean, we don't have to if you don't want to. We can stay here by the fire all night if it's what you would prefer."

"No... um... I want to go for a walk. You just caught me off guard. I think there are owls out there." Adrianna cocked her head and studied him in the firelight, trying to figure out why he was the one speaking so awkwardly. That was usually her job.

"So we shouldn't go for a walk because of owls?" she asked. Greg shook his head. His cheeks were slightly flushed, but Adrianna didn't know if that was just from the heat of the fire he was recently near.

Greg used his plate to gesture toward the woods. "Don't worry about the owls. Yes, let's take a walk, but do you mind if we eat first, so we don't have to carry our garbage with us?"

As they were eating their meal, her eyes widened as she spotted Charles waving at her. He walked over. "Hey! It's Adrianna, the bike rider. How are you doing?"

Adrianna's eyes darted around, trying to make out Dana's form in the darkness. The two people she thought were perfect for each other were in the same place at the same time, but just passing by one another. She really wished she didn't have to worry about confidentiality and could mention how they both had such similar interests. Although, things like that only worked out in her romance books. In the real world, a few similar interests didn't mean that their personalities would mesh. In fact, maybe they'd already met and just didn't feel any chemistry.

Gulping down her food, Adrianna focused on sounding normal and not like a creepy person who knew this guy's background, and had already mentally matched him up with someone he probably didn't know. Being with people was sometimes exhausting. "I'm doing well, although I wouldn't exactly call myself bike-riding Adrianna when I haven't ridden a bike in over a decade other than that day I ran into you."

She pointed to Greg beside her, but when introducing him, she didn't know exactly how to define their relationship. Even though Greg claimed he just wanted to be friends, it sure felt like a lot more. "This is my... friend... Greg. Greg, this is Charles. I ran into him that time you got called into work and I went bike riding."

Greg reached out his hand and shook Charles's. "Good to meet you. Do you live around here?"

Charles nodded. "Yes, I moved nearby recently when I got a job down in the Limestone Vault. I have just been awaiting the completion of my security clearance until I get started. I made friends with Jimmy, and he said I should come and meet some people."

Greg's smile grew. "Well then, I guess I will see a lot of you really soon. I work security there." He pointed to Adrianna. "Adrianna works at BISS Background Investigations. What will you be doing?"

"I am actually going to be starting at BISS, too." He winked at Adrianna. "I look forward to working with you. Maybe we can even go bike riding together next time?"

Adrianna smiled at Charles. "I haven't been working at BISS long, and while there is a big learning curve to get started, so far it seems like a pretty good place to work. I have heard that we are getting so backed up that some investigations are taking months to complete, but when you get started, I'll show you around if you want?"

Greg looked between the two of them and chugged the rest of his drink. "Well, Adrianna and I were just about to go on a walk, if you will excuse us. It was nice to meet you."

Charles raised his eyebrows. "Alright, nice to meet you, too. Bye Adrianna, see you soon."

They threw away their garbage and set off down the path, using their cellphones as flashlights. The path was clear, and there was no sign of the few other couples that she had seen walking down this way. The stars peeked through the trees above, and Adrianna marveled at their gorgeous light against the darkness.

After walking for a while, Adrianna heard an owl hoot, and Greg broke the silence. "So... that guy Charles. I didn't know you found someone else to go bike riding with after I canceled on you. He seems like a nice guy, though."

Shrugging, Adrianna said, "Yeah, he seems nice enough, but I didn't ride with him. Charles is just someone I bumped into on the path."

Greg's shoulders seemed to relax beside her, when she hadn't even realized he was tense. "Do you think you two will hang out more? You will be coworkers soon."

Adrianna glanced over at Greg, wishing she could gauge his expression in the darkness. Was her "friend" jealous? "I'm sure I will bump into him in the future at some point, but I'm in no rush. I'll see him when I see him."

Eventually, the path opened up into a small meadow, with trees surrounding it on all sides. As they stepped out of the woods, Adrianna felt like she had stepped into another world. Everywhere she looked were fireflies, their wings fluttering and blinking in synchronized light in the darkness, a perfect symphony of nature's beauty.

Chapter Twenty-Four: The Case of the Swarming Fireflies

*A*drianna

Adrianna was so captivated by the beauty that she didn't realize that Greg had stopped walking. When she turned around, he was just standing there, watching her with an expression of pure wonderment on his face. She smiled back at him, savoring this moment between them before he spoke again.

"This place is amazing! Look how many fireflies there are! Want to sit down?" He gestured toward a large rock near the edge of the meadow, and Adrianna happily agreed. They sat for a few moments in companionable silence as they watched the fireflies flit around them in the dark.

Adrianna felt an overwhelming desire to kiss Greg burning inside of her, no matter how much she willed it to stay away. Her heart pounded as she leaned closer to him, ignoring her own worries about the consequences of what she was about to do. His warmth drew her in like a magnet, and before either of them had time to think, their lips met in a passionate embrace.

Kissing Greg made every nerve in her body explode like fireworks. He leaned in and hungrily kissed her back, like a man starved for her touch. Their lips moved in rhythm as lights danced about them. Greg moved his hands around her waist, and she arched her back, loving the feel of him. A need for this man was growing deep inside Adrianna, and she realized that she'd never wanted a man more in her life than she wanted Greg right now.

She pressed her body against his hard chest and moved her hand to brush against his cheek. It momentarily surprised her fingers when they ran over the course bumps of his scars. She had all but forgotten about them.

Greg pulled away abruptly, looking stunned. "In all the ways I thought tonight would go, I wasn't expecting you to do that."

Adrianna couldn't find the words to explain what had overcome her. Despite his earlier wishes, there was no way the two of them could go back to the simplicity of friends again. Not when she still wanted him with every fiber of her being.

He definitely seemed to enjoy the kiss too, but he pulled back so abruptly that he must've regretted it. She couldn't look him in the face as she said, "I'm sorry. This place is so romantic, I got caught up in the moment... I know I shouldn't have kissed you."

Mortified that her passions were about to be rejected, Adrianna rose to leave, but his hand closed around hers, and he said, "No, don't go... please stay. Adrianna, I have something I need to confess to you. I can't be your friend anymore. I have feelings for you. More than a friend should like another friend."

Adrianna looked at his face in the moonlight and saw something there that made her heart flutter with anticipation—understanding and kindness, mixed with a hint of desire that made her feel like they could make anything happen together. "I have a confession to make as well. I like you as more than a friend, too."

He held onto her hand and looked up at her with such vulnerability in his eyes. "You're amazing, and I don't want to mess up our friendship. I've wanted to ask you out, but I work such crazy hours, and my scars..."

Leaning down, Adrianna interrupted him with a soft and sensitive kiss. The sensation made her want to dive in more passionately, but she knew they needed to talk first. "I don't even notice your scars anymore, but I actually think they're kind of sexy. They give you a rugged bad-boy look, when I know the man underneath has a heart of gold. I would like to see where things take us if you want to give it a try? It just takes me a while to get really comfortable around people. Do you mind if we take it slow?"

She sat down beside him again, but Greg refused to let go of her hand. "I'm happy to go as fast or slow as you want, but I work long hours at the Vault, and I might get called in for police work in the middle of a date. I really have nothing to offer you."

"All I want is you."

She settled back against his arm, and they stayed there under a starlit sky as fireflies lit up the surrounding darkness.

Chapter Twenty-Five: The Case of the Nosy Friends

Greg walked hand in hand with Adrianna back to the bonfire. He was feeling giddy with the excitement of their new relationship. They had just shared their first kiss, and Greg couldn't help but feel like he was on top of the world.

As they approached the bonfire, Greg could feel Adrianna's grip tighten around his hand. After their last outing together, he could tell she was nervous around new people. A protective resolve settled over him as he prepared to deflect the attention away from her until she became comfortable.

Greg grabbed a drink for himself and Adrianna, and could tell the moment people noticed the two of them were holding hands. His friends were very curious about the girl he'd invited to the bonfire, and Greg and Adrianna were probably gone for their walk in the woods for a long time. This just confirmed what they were all probably thinking and talking about while they were gone.

"Hey, lovebirds!" Jimmy called out. "Looks like someone's got himself a girlfriend!"

Greg couldn't help but smile at Jimmy's teasing. He knew his friend meant well, and he was grateful for the support, but he didn't want to scare off Adrianna.

"Yep, looks like it, and I couldn't be happier," he replied. Instead of wrapping his arm around Adrianna's waist like he wanted to, he grabbed an unopened bag of marshmallows. Food would distract them. "I see someone brought stuff for s'mores. Did you guys want to cook some of these?"

Greg pulled two camp chairs closer to the fire and gestured for Adrianna to sit. She sat down quietly while his friends gathered around. One was cooking some marshmallows and handing out s'mores, but most were laughing and joking as they cracked open another can of beer. Adrianna was sitting next to Greg, her hands folded in her lap, looking nervous.

"So, Adrianna, what do you do for a living?" one of Greg's friends, Ron, asked.

"I'm a background processor at the Vault," she replied softly.

"The Vault, huh?" another friend chimed in. "I've driven near that place a few times, but never had the chance to see beyond the parking lot. I would love the chance to see inside."

Adrianna shifted in her seat uncomfortably. "It's pretty neat going into a deep cave to do paperwork, but I'm getting used to it and it's losing its novelty," she said. Her voice sounded more confident.

"Well, doing paperwork all day sounds boring," Jimmy interjected, taking a swig of his drink. "You must have some more exciting hobbies, right?"

Adrianna shook her head. "I'm pretty boring," she said, a small smile playing at the corners of her lips. "But I love to read a good romance novel."

The conversation continued like this for a while, with Greg's friends asking Adrianna questions about her interests and hobbies. Greg watched her with a fond smile, happy to see her come out of her shell. He knew it could be intimidating to be surrounded by his rowdy friends, but Adrianna seemed to hold her own.

After a while, it seemed her answers became shorter and shorter, so Greg came to the rescue.

He took a swig of his drink and leaned back in his chair, looking around the circle of his friends gathered around the campfire. He took a deep breath and told them a story.

"So, back in the police academy, we had this guy in our class who was always getting into trouble. Let's call him... Joe. Joe was a bit of a troublemaker, to put it lightly."

His friends chuckled and nodded, intrigued.

"One day, we were in our tactics class, and we were learning about how to handle a suspect who's trying to escape. You know, the usual stuff—take them down, cuff them, and all that. Well, Joe volunteered to be the 'suspect' for our class demonstration."

His friends leaned in closer, waiting for the punchline.

"Long story short, Joe tried to run, and our instructor—this big, burly guy—took him down hard. But the thing is, Joe had forgotten to wear his protective gear, so when he hit the ground, he... well, let's just say he had a bit of an accident."

His friends groaned and laughed, shaking their heads.

"Hey, do you guys remember the time we got lost in the woods?" Jimmy asked, grinning.

Greg chuckled. "Oh boy, here we go. Which time?"

Jimmy ignored his friend's teasing and continued, "It was our first camping trip without our parents, and we thought we were so tough. But then we got lost and had no idea what to do."

Adrianna leaned in, interested in hearing the story. "What happened?" she asked.

"We tried to find our way back to camp, but we just kept getting more lost," Jimmy said. "So, we made a shelter out of branches and leaves."

Greg rolled his eyes. "Yeah, our *shelter* was a joke. We might as well have been sleeping on the ground."

Jimmy laughed. "And then we tried to find food. We thought we were survival experts, but we had no idea what we were doing."

Adrianna giggled. "What did you do?"

"We tried to catch fish with our bare hands," Jimmy said, shaking his head. "We were in the middle of the woods with no fishing gear, and we thought we could just grab a fish out of the stream. It was ridiculous."

Greg grinned. "And don't forget about our attempt at starting a fire."

Jimmy laughed. "Oh, that was a disaster. We gathered all these twigs and branches, but we couldn't get a spark to save our lives."

Adrianna couldn't help but chuckle at the image of three teenage boys fumbling in the woods. "What did you end up doing?"

"We ended up sleeping in a pile to stay warm," Greg said, still laughing. "It was a long night."

Jimmy added, "We finally found our way back to camp the next day, but we were starving and exhausted."

Adrianna shook her head in amusement. "You guys were quite the adventurers."

"We were idiots," Greg corrected, grinning.

Jimmy punched his friend in the arm. "Speak for yourself, man."

Greg kept his eyes on Adrianna as she listened intently and even laughed at some of the more ridiculous parts of the story. Greg could see her opening up again. She even joined in with one of her own stories of getting lost in the Vault. It was good to see the people who were important to him getting along.

As the night went on, they all started to drink and joke around. Adrianna seemed to have a good time laughing at their silly antics and sitting around the campfire. His friend Kyle pulled out his guitar and started playing some tunes. Adrianna swayed to the music, smiling. He made a mental note to find out what kind of music she enjoyed.

After a while, Adrianna leaned into Greg and whispered in his ear, "Your friends are really great. I'm glad I came."

Greg smiled at her and pulled her closer, enjoying the warmth of the fire and the company of his friends. Adrianna kissed him. She liked him. She wanted to date him. This night couldn't have gone better in his sweetest daydreams.

As the night wore on, Greg could tell when Adrianna grew tired. When she got up to leave, he walked her to her car, clasping her hand as they said their goodbyes.

"I had a really great time tonight," Adrianna said, smiling up at him.

"Me too," Greg replied, feeling his heart swell with affection for her. "I'm looking forward to seeing you again soon. Say, are you free tomorrow? Can you swim?"

Raising her eyebrows, Adrianna replied tentatively, "Yes, to both. Why?"

Greg flashed one of his brightest smiles. "It'll be a surprise. Just wear a bathing suit under your clothes."

"You're lucky I trust you... I'll be ready." Adrianna leaned in to give him a quick kiss on the lips before turning to get into her car. Greg watched her drive away, feeling a sense of longing in his chest.

As he made his way back to the bonfire, he couldn't help but feel like he was walking on air. He had finally found someone who made him feel alive, and he was excited to see where things would go between them.

"Looks like someone's smitten," Jimmy teased as he approached.

Greg grinned, feeling his cheeks grow warm. "I guess you could say that," he replied.

The rest of the night passed in a blur of laughter and good times, but Greg couldn't stop thinking about Adrianna. He knew that he had found someone special, and he was excited to see where their relationship would go.

As he was packing up to leave, Charles walked over. "Congratulations on the new relationship. It looks like I was just a bit too slow. Make sure you treat her right."

Still able to feel Adrianna's lips upon his own, all Greg could see was a bright future in front of them. "When you find a special woman like Adrianna, you never let her go. I can't imagine a scenario where that would ever change, so don't keep your hopes up."

Chapter Twenty-Six: The Case of the Missing Tubes

A *drianna*

The morning had finally arrived, and Adrianna eagerly waited on her porch, wearing her bikini under her clothes and a towel draped over her shoulder. Today was the first day she would spend alone with her new boyfriend, Greg. No longer hiding behind that friendship label, she was excited to see where things would take them. Adrianna looked around at the flowers swaying from a slight breeze in the sunshine. Whatever he had planned, at least it was warm today.

Greg pulled up in his car, and they both smiled at each other. Adrianna was excited about the adventure he had planned for the day, but she was also feeling a little self-conscious and shy in the daylight after their big kiss. He jumped out of the car and held open her door for her.

Adrianna sat in the passenger seat, fidgeting with excitement. Greg had been secretive about their plans for the day, and it was driving her crazy with anticipation. "Where are we going?" she asked.

Greg just smiled enigmatically. "It's a surprise," he said. "You'll find out soon enough." Adrianna pouted but couldn't help feeling a thrill of excitement. She trusted Greg to plan something amazing for their day together. As they drove, she watched the scenery outside and tried to guess their destination. Suddenly, Greg turned down a gravel road, and Adrianna's heart skipped a beat. She had no idea where they were, and there was nothing around.

"Okay, we're here," Greg said, pulling the car to a stop.

Adrianna looked around, still confused. They seemed to be in the middle of nowhere. All she saw was a river glimmering in the distance. She looked around and back at him. "Are we going swimming in the river? Aren't you afraid we'll get swept down by the current?"

"I'm hoping we get swept down at a nice and slow pace. We're going tubing. It's another local activity that I want you to try, so you can see that there is a ton to do, even though we're in a rural area." He motioned toward the river. "Come on, I tied up some tubes for us down by the bank."

Adrianna eyed the river. She liked the lazy river in the water park near her hometown. How much different could a natural version be? It was a warm and sunny day that seemed perfect for floating along down the river. When they reached the bank, Greg pulled out a bag, and it impressed Adrianna to see that he'd packed everything they needed, including sunscreen, snacks, and plenty of water.

"Ready to hit the water, Adrianna?" Greg asked, grinning. Greg took off his shirt, leaving only his swim trunks, and Adrianna had to force her eyes away from his manly figure.

Adrianna grinned back, saying, "Sure, I'll try it." Slipping down to her bikini, Adrianna's cheeks burned as she felt Greg's eyes on her. Uncomfortable with the scrutiny, she hurriedly climbed into her tube and soon they both pushed themselves off from the shore. The river was cool and refreshing, and the gentle current carried them downstream.

"It's so peaceful here," Adrianna said, closing her eyes and leaning back in her tube.

Greg agreed, saying, "It's the perfect way to relax and unwind." They floated along for a while, chatting and enjoying the beautiful scenery surrounding them. Lush green trees and wildlife surrounded the river, and the occasional splash from a nearby fish added to the ambiance.

As they rounded a bend in the river, the current picked up speed, causing the water to become choppier. Adrianna felt nervous and grabbed onto the handles of her tube tighter. Greg noticed her sudden change in demeanor and asked, "Is everything okay?"

Adrianna nodded, but her knuckles were white from gripping the handles so tightly. "I'm just a little concerned. The water's getting rougher," she said.

"Don't worry," Greg said, reassuringly. "I'm right here with you. I've done this dozens of times, and it will get slightly worse for another few minutes, but then smooth out again." As they continued down the river, the current became even stronger and the water became rougher. Suddenly, Adrianna's tube hit a rock, causing her to lose her balance and fall out of the tube.

"Adrianna!" Greg yelled, watching as the current swept her downstream. Fear clutched her heart as she struggled to stay afloat, but the water swept her along too fast to get any footing. "Help!" she shouted, desperate.

Greg sprang into action, diving off his own tube to catch up to her. "Hang on, Adrianna!" he yelled. The water calmed, and soon Greg could reach her, and they moved closer toward the banks, where they could comfortably stand. Neither of their tubes were in sight.

"I've got you," he said, his voice calm and reassuring after her scare. He held her hand as they walked the rest of the way to shore. Greg helped Adrianna out of the water, and they collapsed onto a large rock. "Are you okay?" Greg asked, his voice full of concern.

Adrianna nodded. "Thank you for coming after me. I'm sorry I lost your rafts."

Greg shrugged. "Of course. Don't worry about the tubes. It was you I was worried about. I'll always be there for you," he said, his hand resting on her shoulder.

After they warmed up in the sun, they made their way back to Greg's vehicle by following the shoreline. Barefoot, Adrianna slipped on a wet and particularly slimy green rock, but Greg was right beside her and caught her. Eventually the tension left Adrianna, and she could chat and laugh with Greg until they made their way back to their things.

They had a few sandwiches Greg had packed for lunch and then took a stroll along the riverbank. They held hands as they walked, enjoying the warmth of the sun and the beauty of the scenery.

"Despite my water mishap, I had a great time today," Adrianna said, breaking the silence.

"Me too," Greg replied. "Would you ever go tubing again? I'll understand if you say no."

Adrianna eyed him, trying to figure out how important floating down a river was to him. "I might give it another shot, but next time I say we use a double raft."

Greg nodded in agreement. "Yeah, that would be fun. We don't have to go rafting again if you change your mind, but I hope you find some things you enjoy doing around here. I know it's nothing like the city, with attractions on every corner. I guess I just hope that you don't get bored with... Hillsboro."

Adrianna's heart skipped a beat. She thought he was going to say he was worried she would get bored with him. While it was an adjustment, she found the place charming and couldn't imagine going back to a life without Greg in it. "I'm falling in love with the place," she said, smiling shyly.

They continued to walk, lost in their own thoughts. As they approached the end of the path, Greg stopped and turned to face Adrianna. As he bent down toward her, Adrianna could feel her heart racing as she became very aware of the broad, muscular chest exposed in front of her. Greg gently placed his hand on the side of Adrianna's face and turned her towards him. She looked deeply into his eyes and saw a mixture of fear and excitement.

"Adrianna, there's something I've been wanting to do all day," he said, his voice barely above a whisper.

Before she could respond, Greg leaned in and kissed her softly on the lips. Adrianna relaxed and responded to the kiss, her arms wrapping around Greg's neck. Her exposed skin brushed up against his with only the thin layers of their bathing suits between them. The kiss was gentle but full of passion, and they both felt a spark of electricity pass between them.

After breaking off the kiss, Greg looked deeply into Adrianna's eyes. In his husky voice, he whispered, "We better get you home."

Chapter Twenty-Seven: The Case of the Mean Grilled Cheese Sandwich

Greg

Greg stood outside the bar, waiting for Adrianna to arrive. Fidgeting with the cuffs of his shirt, he hoped he looked presentable enough for their first real indoor date. He'd promised his friend he would come out and support her singing karaoke tonight, and thought it would be the perfect opportunity to bring Adrianna. He never seemed to want to go somewhere without her anymore.

Just as he was about to check his phone for the tenth time, he saw Adrianna walking toward him. She looked stunning, with her hair cascading down her back and a smile on her face.

"Hey," she said, reaching up to give him a quick peck on the cheek.

"Hi," Greg replied, feeling his heart rate pick up at the sight of her.

As they walked into the bar, the sound of music filled the air. Greg guided Adrianna over to a small table near the stage where his friends had already gathered.

"Hey, man," Jimmy said, giving him a nod. "Nice to see you again, Adrianna."

Adrianna smiled, feeling welcomed by Greg's friends. She scanned the group, her eyes landing on a woman with a microphone in her hand.

"Is that Dana? I didn't realize that was who we were coming to hear," she asked, surprise in her voice.

Greg nodded, grinning from ear to ear. "Yeah, that's her. Just wait until you hear her sing."

Dana stood on the small stage in the dimly lit bar, the microphone in her hand. As the music played, she closed her eyes and took a deep breath. As she sang, the room fell silent. Her voice was hauntingly beautiful, filling every corner of the bar. As Dana's voice crescendoed, the room fell silent. The only sound was the sound of her voice, carrying every word of the song with perfect clarity.

More interested in Adrianna than Dana, Greg looked over to see Adrianna and saw that it entranced her as she swayed to the rhythm of the music. As the last note trailed off, the room erupted into applause. Dana looked out at the crowd, a smile on her face. Greg and his friends cheered, clapping Dana on the back as she made her way back to their table.

"Thanks, guys," she said, a hint of nervousness in her voice.

Suddenly, a man approached the table. Although he looked different by firelight, it surprised Greg to recognize him as Charles. Instead of approaching Adrianna to talk, his eyes focused solely on Dana.

"Excuse me," he said, addressing Dana. "I apologize if I am being too bold, but I just wanted to say that you sang more beautifully than I have ever heard a professional singer. I was wondering if I could buy you a drink, and if you would do me the honor of maybe singing a duet together?"

Dana's cheeks turned pink as she nodded and stood up. She turned to Greg. "Thanks for coming out to support me. It looks like I'll be going back up on stage soon. If I don't get another chance to talk with you, I'll see you at the Vault." She turned to Adrianna and gave her a nod. "Nice to see you again, Adrianna. Greg tells me you work down in the Limestone Vault too. I'll be starting there next week, so maybe we will run into one another."

Adrianna gave a small smile. "Yes, hopefully we will run into one another."

Dana followed Charles to a small table where the two of them ordered drinks and sat huddled together, heads leaned close. After Dana left, Greg looked over at Adrianna, suddenly glad that they were going to get some alone time. Greg took a sip of his drink and decided he didn't want to waste another moment getting to know Adrianna better.

"So, what made you become a background investigator?" Greg asked.

"Technically, I'm just a background processor at the moment. I'm just sorting through people's information, looking for potential issues, but I've always been interested in people, and I wanted to make a difference keeping people safe. I'm not as adventurous as a police officer, but I can keep people's information secure, and make sure that bad people don't get the clearance to be put in positions of high power."

"That's really admirable," Greg said, smiling at her.

A server brought over a large basket of fries covered in cheese sauce and bits of bacon. Adrianna picked one up. "And what do you like to do for fun?"

"I like to hike, fish, and camp. Anything outdoors, really," Greg said.

"That sounds like a lot of fun," Adrianna said, taking a sip of her drink. "I'm more of an indoor person myself. I like to read, and in the past I have dabbled in painting."

"What kind of stuff do you like to paint?" Greg asked, genuinely interested.

"Mostly still lifes, but the flowers near my cottage make me want to give landscapes a try," Adrianna said.

"That's cool. I've always wished I had a talent for painting, but I'm afraid I'm not very artistic," Greg said, chuckling.

"I'm sure you have other talents," Adrianna said, smiling at him.

"Well, I can make a mean grilled cheese sandwich," Greg joked, making Adrianna laugh.

"So, tell me more about your job at the Limestone Vault," Adrianna said, taking a sip of her drink.

Greg leaned back in his chair, a thoughtful expression on his face. "It's a pretty intense job, to be honest. There are a lot of security measures in place, and we have to be on high alert at all times."

Adrianna raised an eyebrow. "That sounds pretty intense. What kind of stuff do you guard?"

Greg hesitated for a moment, his expression growing serious. "I can't really say too much about it, but let's just say it's some pretty high-level stuff. There's a reason the security is so tight."

Adrianna nodded, understanding that there were some things that were better left unsaid.

Greg glanced at the stage and back to Adrianna. "Would you be interested in getting on stage and singing with me?"

Adrianna's eyes grew large, and she adamantly shook her head no.

Greg chuckled. "That's alright, I didn't take you as the type to enjoy the limelight."

They fell into a comfortable silence for a few moments, listening to another singer and simply enjoying each other's company. Maybe he could have a nice relaxing date without having to worry about work for once.

Chapter Twenty-Eight: The Case of the Police Call

*A*drianna

She was thoroughly enjoying her time with Greg at the karaoke bar. He was definitely a people person who needed to be around his friends a lot, but she was feeling like she was okay with that. All that mattered was that she was there with him.

Greg dangled a fry above his mouth and gulped it down with one bite. "These are hitting the spot. Do you like them?"

The fries were good, but Adrianna wasn't particularly hungry. She picked up another one to eat, so he didn't feel like he was eating the entire basket himself. "Yes, very yummy. Although these are hard to eat with all this cheese on them."

As a fry brushed against her lips, she couldn't help remembering his kiss. She wanted more alone time with him where she could get to know the thrill of his gentle touch. Maybe she shouldn't have asked him to take their relationship slow. She was already head over heels.

Adrianna took another bite. "When we're done here, you can come back to my cottage with me and we can put on a movie, if you want?"

Greg gave her one of his bright, broad smiles. "Sure, let me finish my drink and we can head out. What do you want to watch?"

She was a lot less concerned about what was on the television and a lot more hopeful there would be more of those sizzling kisses. "I really only have a few chick flicks, but we can see what's on the television if you want to watch something else."

"Looking forward to it, chick flick or not."

Not long after, she watched Dana following Charles up to the stage. It happily surprised her to see the two of them gravitate toward one another without any nudge from her. Their love of singing karaoke brought them together. They would sure be surprised when they realized they shared a love of sports as well. She just hoped it would be enough. She honestly didn't know enough about either of them to know any more depth to their personalities.

She read some of their deepest secrets, checked their credit reports, and verified their birth certificates, but she realized that there was a lot more to a person than what they could quantify on paper. While she wanted to learn more about Greg, she was thankful to do so the old-fashioned way than to read a report and see if he checked all of her significant-other boxes.

Dana and Charles stood together on the small stage, their voices melding together in perfect harmony. Charles had a deep, resonant voice, while Dana's was higher and more melodic. Together, they created a sound that was pure magic, their eyes locked on one another. As the song progressed, their voices intertwined, each one complementing the other perfectly. They hit every note with flawless precision, their voices soaring together and filling the room with a sense of warmth and joy. Adrianna could see the passion in their eyes as they sang, and she knew they were completely lost in the moment, enveloped in the music. As the song came to a close, the room erupted into applause once again. Adrianna joined in, clapping and cheering as Dana and Charles took their bows.

As they stepped down from the stage, Adrianna caught Dana's eye and gave her a thumbs-up. Dana beamed back at her, clearly thrilled with how the performance had gone. Adrianna couldn't help but notice that Dana and Charles went and sat back down together.

Adrianna turned to Greg and smiled, feeling a sense of warmth and contentment wash over her. This was the night she had always dreamed of, filled with delightful music, good company, and the magic that could only come from the harmony of two people blending together in perfect unison.

"It looks like Dana and Charles are really hitting it off. They sounded wonderful together up there."

Greg nodded, eying up the couple from across the room. "Yes, it seems that way. I don't know Charles that well, but Dana's a great person. I hope he's a good enough guy to deserve her."

While she may not have remembered the details of his credit history, Adrianna remembered reading all the praises of his family and friends in his background investigation. She smiled. "I have a feeling she's in good hands."

Greg raised his eyebrows, but before he could ask her any questions, his phone buzzed. He pulled it out of his pocket to check it. "It's work. Can you give me a second to answer it?"

She nodded, trying to hide her disappointment. "Of course, go ahead. I'll wait here."

Greg stood up from the table and walked away to take the call, leaving Adrianna alone with her thoughts. She wondered what police business it was this time, and for the first time, doubted that she could handle the interruptions that could come at any time. *Was this one a serious crime? Was someone hurt or in danger?* She tried not to let her imagination run wild, but she couldn't help feeling anxious and worried.

A few minutes later, Greg returned to the table, looking grave. "I'm sorry, Adrianna, but I have to go. There's been an incident, and I have to attend to it. It's not something you can tag along for, so I'll drop you off at your cottage on my way."

Adrianna nodded. She understood, but couldn't help feeling disappointed that their time was over. "Okay, I understand. I hope everything is alright."

Greg paid the bill, and the two of them walked to his car in silence. When they arrived at Adrianna's cottage, Greg parked the car and walked her to the door. His eyebrows raised with concern. "I'm sorry our date got cut short, Adrianna. I really had a great time with you tonight."

Smiling, Adrianna tried to hide her disappointment. "I had a great time too, Greg. I'll just look forward to next time."

He nodded, smiling. "I'll be in touch soon. Take care, Adrianna."

Memories of their last epic kiss faded as he leaned in to kiss her goodbye, leaving a small peck, before he turned and walked back to his car, leaving her alone on her doorstep. She watched him drive away, feeling a mixture of disappointment, worry, and fear.

As Adrianna opened the door to her cottage and stepped inside, she couldn't help but wonder what kind of danger Greg was heading into, and if he would be okay? She hoped and prayed that he would return safely, and that their date would continue another time.

She looked over at the spider plant sitting on her kitchen counter. It was drooping and more yellow than green now. "Well, Greg. It looks like it's just you and me tonight. You look horrible. I should probably give you some water."

Chapter Twenty-Nine: The Case of the Missing Waterfall

*A*drianna

After focusing on the pile of paperwork on her desk all morning, Adrianna hopped out of her seat with glee when she realized it was time for her lunch break. Time for a special walk with Greg. She wondered where he would take her and hoped he tried to sneak a kiss.

Grabbing her sandwich bag, she hurried out the door and into the cave. Greg was talking to a man who worked in the room next to hers, but upon seeing her, he excused himself and hurried over with a big smile.

Bouncing on the balls of his feet, he spoke quickly. "So, I have something really neat that I would like to show you today, but we will have to walk really fast if we want to get there and back in only a half-hour. Are you up for it?"

Adrianna nodded her head, trying to imagine what he could be so excited about. "Then I guess we better get started. You can tell me where we're going on the way."

They started walking down a path they took just yesterday, but today Greg took a sharp turn that took them in a completely new direction. "Actually, I'm going to keep it a secret. As far as caves go, this is a pretty boring one, but I'm taking you somewhere that I think is kind of neat."

"You and your secrets and surprises," Adrianna mumbled to herself, but inwardly she was pleased that he was taking the time and energy to think of special places to show her.

The pace they took kept their talking to a minimum. They were moving closer to a slow jog than a walk. Adrianna didn't even bother to open her lunch bag and eat her sandwich today; she could eat at her desk when she got back if she really needed to. She was savoring the energetic walk, and her curiosity was killing her about where Greg was guiding her.

They rounded a corner, and Greg stopped abruptly in front of a blank cave wall and turned to Adrianna to watch her face. Adrianna studied the plain rock. She noted that there were vertical channels cut into it but couldn't find anything out of the ordinary that he would be excited to show her.

She turned toward Greg with her head angled to the side. "Um, this is neat." She waited for Greg to explain, but when he remained silent, she couldn't help but ask, "What exactly are we looking at?"

Greg walked closer to the wall and laid his hand on it. "Do you see these vertical grooves? And on the ground, there is a small channel cut out that leads deeper into the cavern. Well, I think this was once an underground waterfall."

Adrianna leaned forward as she stared at the dry rock and imagined a trickle of water pouring down the wall and into a small stream below. It would have sounded beautiful tinkling against the ground. It may not have been the most majestic waterfall she had ever seen, but it sure was the most unique.

Greg moved back toward her and stood very close. She looked up at him and her heart skipped a beat as the moment she had been hoping for finally came. He leaned down toward her, lips parted. Without warning, the lights went off and submerged her in complete darkness. She gasped in surprise, and she heard Greg ask, "Adrianna? Are you alright?"

Adrianna looked around, and her eyes couldn't make out a single thing. She felt a sudden wave of fear, and her body froze. Everything was darkness. "Yes, I was just surprised. My phone is outside in my car, and I have no other light source. Do you have a flashlight on you?"

In response, Greg clicked on a light, but the pitch darkness surrounding them made her shiver, and she wrapped her arms around herself. Greg put his arm around her shoulders. In that moment, Adrianna realized that with Greg by her side, she was unafraid.

Greg fiddled with the belt on his guard's uniform. "I was just getting mine out. I'm sure glad it's standard issue. Are you sure you're alright?"

Adrianna nodded her head, the movement only barely visible in their limited light. "Yeah, I'm okay. What do you think happened?"

Greg shrugged. "We run landlines down here because walkie talkies and cellphones won't work this deep in the caves. I won't know what's going on until we make our way out of here. I'm sorry, but it looks like you're going to be late getting back to work today."

After Greg took a step forward, Adrianna did as well. She followed his lead, the two of them close together, taking tiny, uncertain steps farther into the darkness, relying on the flashlight beam to find their way back.

"Have the lights ever gone out down here before?"

"Not since I've worked here, but I'm sure it's just a storm outside or some kind of power malfunction. It feels like a lot of things have gone wonky lately."

They were walking so closely together that at one point, their hands brushed against one another. Greg gently clasped her hand and guided her forward. It felt so good and reassuring that Adrianna let him in and held on tightly. He said nothing, but his grip told her everything she needed to know: He would always be there for her, no matter what. She looked up at him, her heart beating faster than ever, and he smiled down at her. In that moment, she felt a deep connection that seemed to stretch further than just this cave.

In the darkness, Adrianna had lost all sense of direction, but Greg seemed to know where he was going, so she put her trust in him not to get them lost. Despite their current atmosphere, Adrianna realized that with him by her side, the world felt like a brighter and warmer place. Together, they could take on anything. For the first time in a long time, she felt like everything was clicking into place.

They walked a good way when Adrianna saw a flash of someone else's light and heard a few muted voices. One voice, a little louder than the others, uniquely slurred his words together. Greg stopped abruptly and tensed up. Instead of calling out to someone else lost in the dark, he turned off his light and squeezed her hand for a moment. She took it as a reassurance but didn't dare ask about his odd actions.

Instead of staying in the center of the walkway, Greg moved toward the direction she thought one of the cave walls was in, and she felt his right arm reach out as if searching for the rock.

She was dying to ask him what was going on, but she was afraid to say a word when he was obviously trying to be stealthy. Together, they silently crept down the tunnel. Hand in hand, they moved forward toward the friend or foe. Adrianna didn't know for sure, but she had a bad feeling. You didn't sneak up on a friend.

Chapter Thirty: The Case of the Missing Information

G^{reg} Greg's heart plummeted as he heard the voice around the bend in front of him. Immediately, he turned off his own light and didn't dare speak. He stood stock still, gently squeezing Adrianna's hand. So she did the same. He waited to see if anyone had heard them or caught a flash of their light and was thankful for the winding maze of tunnels that let them approach, their own light unseen.

He knew that voice and the unique way he slurred his words together. Now he knew for sure that this was no accidental power outage. The Limestone Vault was being broken into, and he and Adrianna were in serious danger. He hoped the other people that worked here were smart enough to stay in their rooms until the power came back on or there would likely be casualties. It was lucky that none of them were allowed to bring phones into the Vault, so unless someone carried around their own personal flashlight, it was likely they would stay put.

During his onboarding training, he was required to watch a series of videos of historical data breaches from other facilities and, as a group, they talked about how each break-in could have been avoided or stopped. There was no mistaking that unique speech pattern. It belonged to a master thief that managed to always get away.

When he started working in security, Greg had spent his time studying technology and valuable heists, but sometimes the hardest ones to prepare for were when only information was trying to be stolen. There was a lot of valuable data down here that could only be accessed from the inside on secure servers, but he had no clue which kind of information or which room they would be accessing. He was kicking himself for not taking those recent security glitches seriously. Apparently, this heist had been planned for a while now, and he was being too complacent and focused on Adrianna to take note.

Before he could take care of the intruders, he had to get Adrianna somewhere safe. He couldn't do his job while worrying about her safety, and he had to admit that her wellbeing was now more important to him than anything else in the world. He put away his flashlight and used his spare hand to feel his way along the rock wall as he walked.

As he held Adrianna's hand tightly with his other hand in the cool dark cavern, he mourned their lost moment of intimacy, feeling her warm body pressed against his own in front of the dry waterfall. He yearned for the carefree feeling of new beginnings as she fervently kissed him like she did in the firefly-lit meadow, but for now, he had to push those feelings away. That would have to wait.

He pictured a map of the caves in his mind and tried to imagine where they were. Luckily, part of his training when he started here was memorizing these caves, but he had never needed to navigate them in the darkness before. He worked with an entire team of highly specialized security personnel. He wished he had a way to reach them and find out how these crooks had made it inside. Before today, he would have said it was nearly impossible.

The question was, should he and Adrianna try to leave through the entrance to get outside help, or stay in the mine to be the most effective? A plan formed in his mind. The thieves would probably be stationed at the main entrance, keeping their escape route clear, but if Greg got to the underground bunker, there was a generator he could turn on, and he could stash Adrianna in a safe place. There were controls he could use to auto lock all the inner doors in the cavern, so the civilians stayed safe inside, even after they got restless. The lockdown would also keep the burglars from being able to steal anything. There was also a communications room where he could call in reinforcements, even when the rest of the facility was out of power.

Greg gave a quick squeeze to Adrianna's hand as he moved along the cave wall. He hoped she understood the seriousness of their situation and didn't talk. He didn't dare whisper to tell her what he knew. Greg navigated Adrianna through the darkness of the cave, staying close to the walls. He could hear the footsteps and muffled voices of the burglars echoing off the stone walls. He remained alert, ready to respond if they were discovered.

The two of them slowly made their way through the winding tunnels, inching closer to safety. Greg could feel his heart pounding in his chest as they heard a voice echo from around the corner. He immediately put a finger to Adrianna's lips and motioned for her to get down and be still. The beam of the flashlight ahead of them was strong enough that he knew it would betray them if they moved, so he hoped Adrianna would stay put as he tried to figure out what was going on up ahead.

Luckily, after a few moments of tense waiting, it seemed like the voices were leaving, and they could make their escape without being noticed.

Greg led Adrianna as they silently zigzagged through the dark passageways, cautiously avoiding any open areas as much as possible. Their heavy breathing was the only noise that Greg could hear, but he felt his heart pounding with fear and adrenaline. Finally, after what felt like an eternity, they made it to the entrance of the underground bunker.

Greg swiped his security badge and slowly opened the door, making sure not to make any sound. They both peered inside to find a small room illuminated by emergency lights in the corner. He entered first and quickly pulled Adrianna inside with him before anyone could notice them in the entranceway.

Once inside, Greg released Adrianna's hand and quickly surveyed their surroundings. He watched as Adrianna gaped at what looked like a large living room in the middle of a cave to their left and the rows and rows of supplies to their right. There was a large generator in one corner, and he knew that this was where the Vault kept their backup power source for emergencies like this one. He could also see a control panel with several buttons that he assumed controlled various locks throughout the caves.

He furrowed his brows while he examined the panel. He figured out the specifics of the equipment quickly, thanks to the well-labeled components. It didn't take long to figure out what each button did, and after pressing several of them, Greg was satisfied that he'd securely locked down all access points in The Limestone Vault until further notice.

Finally breaking their silence, he said, "Come on, I just locked everything down, so you should be safe in here, but we need to act quickly. We need to get to the communications room and call for backup. I don't know exactly what these guys are trying to steal, but they warned me in training about potential data thieves. I recognized the voice of the man we heard in the hallway."

Greg could hear the stress in Adrianna's voice, and he wished he could immediately ease all her fears. "How can help get in here if you locked everything down? Who are those people out there?"

"His name's Joshua, and he's a thief that steals information to sell on the black market. The employees down here are in grave danger because he and his team won't hesitate to kill anyone in their path, but don't worry. There is a back door I can use to let in help."

Wide-eyed, Adrianna stayed silent and just nodded her head. He knew he had to act fast if they were going to get out of this alive, so he grabbed her hand one last time and started sprinting down the hall to find the communications room. He had expected as much, but it was still a relief that the room was fully functional thanks to some backup generators; now all they had to do was contact security so help could come in time.

He was swiping his badge to enter the communications room when he felt a gun press against the small of his back.

Chapter Thirty-One: The Case of the Presidential Suite

A *drianna*

Adrianna held her breath, the sound of her hammering pulse thrumming in her ears. She felt an icy dread that sent a shiver up her spine when a gravelly voice behind her spoke. "Put your hands on your heads if you want to live to see tomorrow."

Her heart had been racing as she and Greg had skulked through the darkness, but this was a different fear. She slowly turned around, her hands trembling as she prepared for the worst.

But instead of the twisted figure of a monster, Adrianna saw a tall, broad-shouldered man wearing a guard's uniform very similar to Greg's. He held a flashlight loosely in one hand and a gun pointed straight at them in the other. His expression was stony as he stared her down.

Adrianna's mind raced. Was this man a criminal in a guard's uniform? The man watched her intently, waiting for a response. Adrianna swallowed hard before slowly raising her hands and resting them on her head, and she saw Greg do the same out of the corner of her eye. The man from behind them kept the gun pointed at them while he patted down Greg and emptied every tool from his guard's belt.

The man quickly patted down Adrianna, but when he found nothing useful, he pushed her forward as he kept his gun on Greg. "Alright, tell me what you're doing here."

"Jeremy, we're here to call in reinforcements," Greg said warily. "What are you doing back here?"

Jeremy's expression softened slightly, and he nodded. "I heard a strange noise, and I came to investigate. I didn't know you were here." He gestured with his gun at Adrianna. "Who is this?"

"This is Adrianna," Greg said firmly, stepping forward protectively as he gestured to her. "She's with me. You don't have to worry about her. She works down here on background investigations."

Jeremy sighed wearily before speaking again. "Alright, I just wanted to make sure which side you're on. I just came from the communications room. Someone destroyed all the equipment inside. I think the thieves have an inside man."

He holstered his gun and gave them a small smile that didn't reach his eyes. "Well then, let's get you both out of here." He began leading them back toward the entrance. Adrianna let out a relieved sigh, thankful that they were both safe and had found an additional ally. She looked at Greg, who smiled down at her, and she couldn't help but feel grateful for his presence.

They walked back to the room that was decorated like a large living room, containing couches with rugs. "Why do you think there's an inside man?" Adrianna asked, feeling her heart rate increase as she thought about their situation.

"Someone connected to this facility must be helping them," Jeremy replied grimly. "It's the only way they could know where the equipment is and how to disable it. They came in through the back door, and as we both know, that door can only be opened from the inside." He shook his head in frustration before continuing. "We need to get back above ground so we can report this and get backup."

He turned toward Adrianna and Greg, his expression unreadable. "You two stay together and follow me," he commanded, before picking up his brisk pace, leaving Adrianna and Greg to scramble after him.

Jeremy turned toward a doorway that ran off the living room area of the cave. He gestured for them to walk as he talked. "I picked up about a dozen people roaming the tunnels on my way here. I was planning on getting outside help, just like you were."

Through the doorway, Adrianna entered an expensively furnished and elaborately decorated suite. Most of the rooms she had gone into in the Vault had cubicles and a few drywalled offices built right against the rock wall. While painted with a thick white paint, she had become accustomed to seeing exposed rock ceilings and floor. This room was unique. The interior designer of this room made sure that every inch was perfectly trimmed and decorated with an excessive amount of lighting, so you couldn't even tell that you were underground.

Each light fixture was an artistic rendition of some sort of eagle, falcon, or other large bird of prey, its claws gripping the sides of the fixture, its eagle head and wings spread wide, like they were flying or diving. It was beautiful.

Stone floors and walls gave way to a thick carpet and smooth dry-wall. They had placed an expansive bar along an entire side of the room, with a lounge area on the other side. Adrianna's eyebrows shot upwards as she surveyed the scene.

An enormous stone fireplace spread out opposite the bar. It was huge, and she could imagine it would make the room quite cozy with an electric fire glowing within, throwing off a welcome warmth into the room.

Greg was looking around, as if taking everything in as he spoke. "I see you brought everyone into the presidential vault. That was good thinking. We can lock this down. It's the most secure place in these caverns if we run into trouble. Unfortunately, that doesn't help the several hundred other people working down here. I secured most of them in their rooms now, but that only bought us a bit of time and didn't help anyone who was traveling in the tunnels when the lights went out. If there is no help on its way, it looks like we have to figure this out on our own. Jeremy, I'm glad I have you here to come up with a plan. I always admired your ability to solve potential issues when we were trained together. You know what Joshua's crew is looking for?"

Jeremy's eyes rose in surprise. "You know who's doing this? That's good to know. I'm not sure exactly what they're after, but the guys I saw were headed toward a room owned by the Department of Defense, so it can't be anything good."

Adrianna smelled coffee a moment before they walked into a large dining room. A second guard and eleven faces turned toward them as they entered. Each person was sitting around a round table with an assortment of prepackaged foods in front of them. She didn't recognize any of them, except Judy.

Greg nodded his head at the guard in the corner, then went around and immediately got to work writing down everyone's name and departments, so she walked over to her coworker. "Judy, are you alright?"

Judy nodded her head. "I guess so. At least they are letting us have something to eat as we're kept here. They picked you up, too? This is what we get for taking a late lunch, but I never thought they would take me hostage for it."

Adrianna cocked her head in puzzlement and then turned toward the doorway. Jeremy had a gun pointed straight at Greg.

Chapter Thirty-Two: The Case of the Failed Test

Greg groaned as he looked up to see a gun pointed at him yet again. He had been so trusting, expecting a friendly face this time, but should have been suspicious when Jeremy never handed him back his gun. The guard in the room's corner was one he hadn't worked with before. The fellow had just finished training recently, and Greg couldn't remember his name.

The guard had a gun in his hand too and was pointing it at Greg. Greg felt himself tense up, and he looked around the room. He was alone in a room full of civilians, and the situation was becoming more dire by the second.

Assessing the room, Greg knew he couldn't take on both armed men, especially with so many civilians in the room, too. He focused on Jeremy, his voice hard. "You're the inside man. Why did you try to trick me?"

Jeremy sighed, but didn't look perturbed. "When I saw it was you, I had to think of some way to convince you to come down here with the other hostages. I couldn't risk hand-to-hand combat, because you always beat me when we trained together. I'll shoot you if I have to, but I am giving you a chance to let us wrap up our business down here for old times' sake."

Greg glanced over at Adrianna but never fully let Jeremy out of his sight. She looked like all the blood had drained from her face as she, too, was coming to terms with their predicament. "Jeremy, why would you help someone like Joshua? I thought you were a standup guy. A friend."

Jeremy's gravelly voice was suddenly getting on Greg's nerves like it never had before. "Are you willing to pay me three million dollars to be your friend? Joshua is. All I had to do was open a door, destroy a bit of equipment, and keep a few hostages silent while Joshua picks up a little dongle to get behind the Department of Defense's firewall. Then I'm rich and off to a beautiful beach, where I can bask in the sunshine at my leisure instead of working long hours in the depths of a cave."

At this, Greg felt the hostages murmur in fright.

Jeremy threw up his hands defensively and paced around the room. "Listen, I don't want anyone to get hurt here. I don't know Joshua very well, but he offered me a lot of money for essentially doing a few simple tasks. A few million dollars is more than I could ever make in my entire lifetime" His eyes focused on Greg. "Besides, this job is killing me. Day in and day out, it's the same thing over and over again. Staring at a bunch of screens watching everyone else go about their everyday lives. I couldn't stand it anymore, and frankly, it's rather annoying how cheerful you remain, Greg."

Greg ground his teeth and said under his breath, "I'm keeping people safe from people like you."

Jeremy stared at Greg for a moment, then without responding, he let out a loud sigh before continuing, "I came up with an idea that would keep everyone safe. It won't be easy, but it will ensure that no one gets hurt." He pointed toward Adrianna and nodded at her before looking back at the other hostages.

"The plan is simple," he said. "I need a background investigator to log onto your database and download all the personal investigations for the people in this room. I know there are at least a few of you in this room. I know I can't force your fingers to type in passwords, so one of you can either volunteer to do this for me, or I shoot people."

Greg's voice growled as he responded, "Do you really think you won't have any consequences after this? These are people's lives you are ruining. What do you want us to do for you anyway?"

Jeremy sighed and looked around at the frightened faces in the room. "This isn't about what you are going to do for me today, but for Joshua in the future. Blackmail isn't ideal, I know, but it is effective, and giving me what I want is the only way to ensure that no one gets harmed here today." He nodded around the room and looked back at the group. "Who is ready to help me?"

Fury like he'd never felt before built inside of Greg. He couldn't believe this man he called his friend would bring innocent people into this. Why in the world would Joshua want the background information for a random group of people that worked down here? He looked around the room and recognized people from a broad range of fields. Jeremy was probably just wasting their time until the job was complete. He was keeping them busy with a promise of freedom so that no one tried anything heroic. He hoped no one fell for it.

The room was silent as everyone was stunned by Jeremy's proposal. No one seemed willing to accept his offer.

With two guns pointed straight at him, Greg stood stock still, staring death straight on. He was a man of honesty and integrity. No matter the consequences, he wouldn't play any of their games. He had come to peace that he would put his life on the line when he got into this profession, and it had never bothered him until he met Adrianna. If something happened to him, he would really miss what could have been. He felt like there was something real between them.

Greg heard the click of Jeremy cocking the gun straight at his head. Immediately, Adrianna stepped forward. "I'll do it," she said.

Chapter Thirty-Three:
The Case of the Sleeper Cell

*A*drianna

Trying to hide the shaking of her hands, Adrianna stood up straight in front of Jeremy. "What do you need me to do?"

Jeremy walked over to a bag in the room's corner and pulled out a laptop. He sat it on the table in front of where Adrianna sat. "I thought if I kept this gun pointed at Greg, you might volunteer. You two looked pretty chummy. Take a seat. You have work to do."

Adrianna sat down in front of the laptop, but kept her hands on her lap. Jeremy raised his voice. "Don't just sit there, start typing. You are about to log into the personal background investigation of everyone in this room. I'm going to send it to Joshua's servers so he knows what will cause everyone here the most pain if you don't comply."

Adrianna sat frozen, not wanting to hand over confidential information to these criminals, but also very aware of the consequences for not doing as he said. Jeremy waved the gun toward Greg. "Why don't you start with your own information? I might need to find something else to convince you with if you don't hurry, and I end up needing to dispose of Greg here."

Adrianna logged in. It was easier to give away her own life story than the ones others trusted her with. She would give them access to every detail she held dear. They would know everything from her love of romance novels to the addresses of her closest family members. The thought made her balk at continuing forward, but she needed to buy herself some time to figure a way out of this.

She could feel Judy's silent glare from beside her, but she truly didn't know what else to do. If she didn't do what they asked, people would start losing their lives. She tried to make eye contact with Greg across the table, but only received an expressionless stare. She hoped he didn't hate her after this, but if it meant he got to keep his life, she refused to regret it.

After pulling up her own report, Jeremy copied the data file. He laid a piece of paper down in front of her and added Greg's name to the list. "These are the rest of the names you need to look up. Lucky for you, we were taking roll call just before you arrived. Add these files just as I showed you. If any are missing, remember that we now have all of your personal information to make sure you regret it."

Jeremy looked at his phone and took another piece of paper out of his bag. "Well, it looks like we only have a few more moments together, so we need to get started on the next part while Adrianna is busy ruining the safety of all your lives."

He laid a piece of paper in the middle of the table. "We're going to talk about communication. A message may come in a few months after the dust settles from this heist or in twenty years when one of you is in a unique position of power. Regardless, whenever Joshua needs you to do something, he will not call you or send a letter. He sends ciphers to his agents."

A man sitting in the corner scrunched up his facial features before asking, "What happens if we refuse to do what the puzzles say?"

Bang! Adrianna jumped in her seat. She hadn't even seen as Jeremy quickly lifted his gun and shot into the wall beside the man's head. The man turned white and shook, but didn't say another word. "I will let your own imaginations guess at what will happen to whoever or whatever you care about if you get lazy and miss or ignore a message. Just believe me, whatever Joshua does will be worse. Any other questions, or can we get down to business?

"As I was saying, your message will arrive as some sort of puzzle that you will have to decipher in order to understand your full instructions. You will also find a written key delivered in some kind of ubiquitous way as well, such as a love letter from someone we find in your file. Joshua's favorite cipher right now is one that contains two very similar fonts broken into groups of five. Each combination of type creates a different letter. For example, in a fake message from your spouse, the words 'I love you' might mean something completely different because the first three letters are in font A and the next two are font B. Depending on the font combination and your written key, you can decipher each group of letters to decode the hidden message."

Jeremy walked over and looked briefly over Adrianna's shoulder. He took a second to check that she had finished and then closed the laptop, pulled out a small data drive, and stuck it in his front shirt pocket before shoving the laptop back in his bag. "It looks like everyone here gets to live to see another day. You have just changed from liabilities to assets.

"A parting word. Remember that I now have access to all of your personal information. I will know where you live, where you like to go, what you like to do, who you are married to. You will do exactly as I say, or else there'll be serious consequences for you and your loved ones." He pointed his gun at each one of them so that they understood the consequences.

A shiver ran down Adrianna's spine, but she couldn't help but let out a sigh of relief that at least this part was over. They were packing up to leave and everyone was still alive.

He slung the bag over his shoulder and nodded his head toward the door to his co-conspirator in the corner. "I would suggest doing some research on codes and puzzles before you need it. Joshua is constantly changing his methods and getting more creative in how he delivers them, so from now on, you need to check not just every paper, but everything that comes into your personal and work life very carefully. Believe me, you and your loved ones' lives depend on it."

The two men started to slowly walk backwards toward the door while keeping their guns pointed at them. She watched Greg, whose muscles were tensed, as if he planned to jump into action as soon as the two men were out of his line of vision.

Jeremy waited until the other man left. Holding the door, he looked around the room at each of them and smiled. He never let his gun waver, but as he was closing the metal door, he said, "Congratulations, you are now Joshua's new sleeper agents."

Chapter Thirty-Four: The Case of the Angry Policeman

G *reg*

Flying out of his seat, Greg yanked on the doorknob as soon as Jeremy shut it. He let out a frustrated growl. Jeremy had locked it. Those backstabbing crooks would escape while he sat helpless, locked in one of the most secure places in the world.

Everyone in the room got up out of their seats and were slowly mingling, except for one woman who moved to a corner, hunched over crying. A few people searched the room. He saw Adrianna walk over and try to comfort the woman, but when the woman gave her the cold shoulder, she approached him. He was so relieved she was safe, but he had no clue what to say to her right now. She gave away information that turned every person in this room into a target, and she did it all for him. He didn't want these people to live in fear because of him. It was just too much guilt.

He admitted to himself that he might have done the same thing if the tables were turned, but right now, he didn't have the mental power to focus on what happened a few minutes ago. He had to figure out a way to get them out of this safely, so he could start tracking down Jeremy and Joshua.

Everyone gave Adrianna a wide berth as she made her way to Greg, and he caught a few people outright glaring at her. She looked up at him with her beautiful, wide eyes. "Greg, I'm sorry..."

Interrupting her, Greg shook his head. "We will have time to talk about this later. Right now, I need to focus on being the Vault's security personnel and get these people to safety. Do you have any ideas?"

Someone hunched over and looking into one of the bottom cupboards in the room yelled out, "Hey, I think there is a little door down here!"

Greg hurried over and threw a few things out of the cabinet so that he had enough leverage to open the door. Greg really wished he still had his flashlight. It was a narrow black hole scarcely wide enough for a large man to climb through.

Standing up, Greg spoke to the entire group, trying not to make eye contact with the woman of his dreams. She looked like she was trying to hold back tears. All he wanted to do at that moment was comfort her and assure her that everything would be alright, but he didn't have time for that right now.

He cleared his throat. "Pay attention, everyone. I want you guys to barricade the door just in case someone tries to come back in here. I am going to see if this tunnel leads somewhere that I can get help. Put a barricade up behind me and stay prepared in case I need to return this way. I will give a series of five knocks with a brief pause and then two more so that you know it's me."

Greg saw the group immediately take action, pulling tables, chairs, and cabinets toward the door. The adrenaline must've still been coursing through their systems. He knelt down, took a deep breath, and crawled into the pitch-dark tunnel. It was cement, and other than scuffing his uniform, he felt no water or debris that led him to believe he was crawling toward danger. In all honesty, it wouldn't have surprised him if there was a secret passageway going to the presidential suite. He couldn't imagine where else it would head toward.

Unable to see anything, his other senses seemed to sharpen. He heard shuffling and paused, knowing he wasn't alone in here. A moment later, someone banged into his feet, and he recognized Adrianna's voice, pitched higher than normal, as she said, "Sorry!"

Greg couldn't help but let out an enormous sigh of relief that it wasn't a giant rat. Then he tensed back up as his fear for her safety came rushing toward his senses. "Adrianna! What are you doing here? You should be safely back with everyone else. It's going to be dangerous out there."

Adrianna said nothing at first, but he heard her speak softly, but firmly. "I need to help wherever I can. I feel like a traitor, and I need to make it right. Please, let me come with you."

The tunnel was too narrow to turn around, and Greg felt a pang of guilt that she felt like a traitor because she had saved his life not twenty minutes ago. He remembered the look in Jeremy's eyes when he held that gun at him. They may have been friendly at one time, but he had chosen his side and was fully committed to Joshua, or at least the money Joshua was going to give him.

Starting back up his crawl, Greg whispered in case this tunnel carried their voices. "Alright, but you will have to listen to everything I tell you. If I ask you to stay behind or hidden at any point in time, you will. You're not a traitor, you just did what you felt you needed to in a stressful situation. We will get all of that sorted out later, but right now, I can't bear to let anything happen to you."

They shuffled along in silence for long enough that Greg worried. If the door on the other side didn't open, it would be really hard to crawl backwards the whole way out of here, and he would have lost so much time. His shoulders were cramping, his knees sore, and he shivered from either a real or imagined spider dropping into his hair. Would they even be able to get out of this if they had to return to that door? He asked the hostages to secure it. What if they eventually assumed he made it out the other side? A panic he'd never felt before grew in him until he started wishing he could crush his way out of this tunnel. His breathing was beginning to come in fast, shallow gasps as he tried to keep himself calm. He stayed silent, so he didn't worry Adrianna, but he *needed* out of this tunnel.

Greg had never felt claustrophobic before, but he'd also never crawled through a skinny, pitch-black tunnel underground. He was worried if they kept going like this that he would pass out, and he didn't want to do that to poor Adrianna, who was trustingly following only a few feet behind him. Maybe he should tell Adrianna that they needed to turn back. He couldn't do this anymore.

To his surprise, a moment later, he felt a sharp pain course through his head as he heard his skull thunk into the metal door in front of him.

Chapter Thirty-Five: The Case of the Big Red Bed

A^{drianna}

Adrianna bumped into the back of Greg's shoes yet again. "Everything alright up there?"

There was a pause, and then she heard him breathe heavily as he spoke. "Yeah, I think we made it to a door. I should have examined the other door more closely before entering these tunnels. It's just hard to figure out how to open it in the dark."

Adrianna kept herself silent as she heard Greg fumble with something. During her regular days of working in the Vault, she thought she'd yearned for the sunshine. A few minutes in a creepy pitch-black tunnel made her skin feel like she needed to feel its rays. She would never take light for granted again. Even a tiny flashlight would be such a relief right now.

She was wondering what they would do if Greg couldn't figure out how to get the door open? What if the door was locked? In this skinny tunnel, she certainly couldn't get around him to help. She would have to wait and be patient. She had no fears about backing out of this tunnel if they needed to, but the sound of Greg's heavy breathing really bothered her. It sounded like he was doing something really strenuous when all they did was climb through this tunnel for about two minutes.

She jumped in her skin as Greg's sound of triumph reverberated off the walls. "Ah-ha! I got it." Light shone into the tunnel, making her blink hard. Without another word, Greg tumbled out of the tunnel faster than she could have imagined him to move in such a small space.

She followed close behind, her eyes adjusting to the light. When she crawled out, she looked around, puzzled that there was a ceiling right above them. Then it dawned on her. They were under a gigantic bed. She saw Greg's form disappear until all she could see were his shoes. It looked like he was hopping.

Adrianna crawled out from beneath the bed, her eyes wide with awe and wonder. She had never seen such luxury in her life—they'd decorated the room with antiques and regal furniture, the floor adorned with a rich, ruby-red carpet that seemed to go on forever. In the center of the room was a grand canopy bed, covered in thick blankets and pillows of every hue.

Adrianna felt as though she had stepped into a different world, one far removed from the drabness of the cave system in which she had been working. She couldn't fathom how such extravagance could exist in a place where there was no natural light.

Fortunately, no one else was in the room except for her and Greg. She cocked her head as she watched Greg. He was doing jumping jacks, his brow wet with sweat. "So... are we trying to catch some bad guys, or starting our morning workout?"

Greg stopped the jumping jacks and shook out his body. When he spoke, he didn't make eye contact. "I'm sorry. I just needed a moment to stretch."

He took a deep breath, relaxed his muscles, and smiled. He took a few steps toward Adrianna and placed his hands on her shoulders while he looked down at her. "I appreciate that you want to be brave, but I will move more quickly if you stay here. It should be pretty safe here, and you can always crawl back through the tunnel under the bed if you hear someone coming in."

Leaning down, Greg planted a kiss on her forehead. "I'm heading to the armory and the communications room. Stay safe."

He let her go and moved to the door, but Adrianna followed close behind him. She couldn't let the man she was falling in love with risk his life with no backup. Besides, she felt the need to do something. She'd felt so helpless sitting at the table as Jeremy forced her to share her private information. It made her angry that he was trying to use her life's history to blackmail her into being Joshua's sleeper agent. She refused to sit here and be a scared victim. She needed a chance to take her life back.

She set her jaw, and Greg frowned. "You aren't going to stay, are you?"

Adrianna shook her head without explaining. He could argue anything she said. He might try to convince her to stay safe. Maybe he would even succeed. It was far better to stay quiet in order to win the argument before it even began.

With an exaggerated sigh, Greg moved toward the door, motioning her to follow. "If you are coming, stay close and be silent. You never know when we will have to duck into a room at the last minute. The armory is close by, just down the hallway. With any luck, it will be untouched, since it isn't the target for this operation."

Plastering himself against the wall, he motioned for her to do the same before he slowly inched the door open. When it was wide enough for him to fit through, he checked both ends of the hallway before waving for her to follow.

Following Greg closely, Adrianna tried to walk as quietly as she could. She heard a noise farther down the hallway, and before she knew what was happening, Greg pulled her into a nearby darkened room and held her close to his chest. Neither of them moved as she listened, but Greg's manly odor as he clutched her to him was distracting. His shirt was slightly damp against her face, but she could hear his heart race and felt everywhere that his skin touched her own.

She felt that if the day had gone differently, the dark room would have had an entirely different vibe than a few minutes of refuge. She ached to kiss him once this was all over, yet she honestly didn't know if they would remain friends.

I am a traitor now.

Chapter Thirty-Six: The Case of the Cavalry

*A*drianna

Adrianna watched as Greg stopped at a door with a retinal and fingerprint scanner. A large door opened, and they stepped inside. Greg and Adrianna had reached the armory, a large and dusty room packed with guns, knives, and other weapons she had only ever seen in movies. Greg looked around with a wide grin on his face and selected what seemed to be an appropriate arsenal. Adrianna hung back and watched, feeling slightly lost and hopelessly out of her depth.

Adrianna reached for a taser gun, but Greg stopped her hand. "A taser is dangerous and too hard to aim." He handed Adrianna a billy club instead. Adrianna held it loosely. *Did he expect her to beat someone up with this?* He was already moving toward the door, so instead of arguing, she just followed. It was probably for the best. At least she couldn't accidentally shoot Greg with only a stick in her hands.

When they had finished stocking up, Greg motioned for her to follow him. He was much more confident now with a gun in his hands. Adrianna followed closely behind. She felt a strange combination of fear and relief. She was sure Greg knew what he was doing, but there was something about being in such a dangerous situation that made all the rational parts of her shut down in favor of pure instinct.

Adrianna stayed silent as they stealthily walked farther down the hallway, and Greg let them in the communications room. Inside were computers and all sorts of electronic devices that she couldn't identify. Not that it really mattered. Someone had smashed all the electronics into little pieces. Greg walked over to a machine that was still showing words on part of the screen. He started typing away, obviously knowing what he was doing, even without seeing everything he did. He shook his head. "Jeremy was sure thorough in destroying things in here. I doubt this will do anything, but I'm going to send out an SOS in the off chance that it can still make it to the outside world. Most likely, though, we are on our own unless we run into some other guards that Joshua hasn't turned."

Was it really just today that they were visiting a dried-up waterfall? She felt like she had her entire life ahead of her, but now everything seemed to be crumbling to pieces.

Greg must have noticed her pause because he put his hand on her shoulder and said, "It's time to go." She nodded, then followed him.

Adrianna trailed behind him silently, her mind whirling with emotions and questions. *What were they going to do? Where would they go from here? Were they just going to ignore what happened today?* Sadly, even though this was the perfect job for her, there was no way she could continue working on background checks after today's events. BISS would surely revoke her security clearance, and she couldn't risk Joshua holding blackmail over her head any longer.

But then what about Greg? She hadn't known him long, but already he was much more than just an acquaintance to her. She had seen his tough exterior crack since coming here, and it seemed like maybe there might be a real connection between them. But she knew that if he found out about her working with Joshua, even involuntarily, it would certainly be the end of whatever relationship they had budding between them.

The thought of leaving this town behind filled Adrianna with sadness and dread. Just yesterday, it felt like everything in life was finally looking up for her—she had a great job, a newfound relationship with Greg, and optimism for the future ahead of her. And now it would all be gone...

They walked in silence, their footsteps echoing down the corridors as they looked for a way out. Adrianna gripped her billy club tightly, her knuckles pale and her stomach in knots.

They made their way out of the presidential suite and then out of the secure bunker. The lights were back on. Were the criminals gone already? There was no sign of which direction they should head, so Adrianna waited to see what Greg would do.

He leaned back and whispered in her ear, "Everyone might be gone, but we are going to head to the front entrance to get help. We are going to stay close to the walls and stay silent."

Adrianna nodded and followed Greg's lead as he crept along the walls with his gun raised. The pair carefully moved from one cave wall to another until they finally reached the front entrance of the Vault. Adrianna held her breath as she peered around the last corner before the entrance. It was dark, but she could make out two figures in the distance.

Greg held her back with his hand and mouthed, "Wait." She nodded, feeling very unprepared as she hefted her stick around, trying to get a good feel for it. After what felt like an eternity, Greg nodded his head and slowly and quietly made his way to the entrance.

Adrianna watched closely as Greg moved, motioning for her to stay. He was walking lightly, and she hoped he wouldn't make a noise to alert the two figures in front of them. As they got closer, Adrianna could make out that one of them was Jeremy, and the other man was the silent one who was in the room with them earlier. From this angle, she could see that he had several guns strapped to his belt, which made her heart beat faster. She must have missed them when she first thought he was on their side and then was working on the computer.

Adrianna gasped in shock as she witnessed a group of men wearing masks and black uniforms swarm into the room. Before she could even blink, one of them had thrown a small ball toward them. Her ears rang and everything went dark.

She couldn't see anything, and her heart was pounding wildly with fear. She knelt down against the wall, trying to make herself as small of a target as possible. *Who were these people and what did they want? Was this some kind of additional attack or the cavalry?* She tried to focus on interpreting the surrounding noise when she jerked backwards at a touch.

Chapter Thirty-Seven:
The Case of the Flash Drive

Adrianna

Adrianna slowly opened her eyes as the world swam back into focus. The ringing in her ears dissipated, replaced by Greg's voice, reassuring and steady. "It's all over now. The FBI is taking over." Relief washed over Adrianna, and she shivered as Greg wrapped his arms around her protectively. She clung to him, a tear escaping down her cheek. *Would this be the last time he held her like this?*

Adrianna noticed Jeremy, not too far from them, causing a commotion as he surrendered to the authorities. Police officers and FBI agents, their guns trained on him, surrounded Jeremy. He shouted angrily, "I can't believe Joshua would abandon me just because I was a minute or two late to our rendezvous. I got what he wanted." Adrianna watched as they patted Jeremy down and took the small data drive from Jeremy's shirt pocket.

The special agents continued to speak with him, their words blending together in the chaos. Greg's voice cut through the noise, drawing her attention back to him. "Adrianna, are you okay?" His face was pale, as if he had seen a ghost.

"I think so," she croaked, her voice hoarse. "What's going on?"

"It's Jeremy," Greg explained, his voice tense. "He didn't get out with our personal information, but Joshua's gone."

Adrianna shook her head, trying to make sense of it all. "What are they going to do to Jeremy?"

Greg shrugged. "I'm not sure. All I know is they're taking him away."

Adrianna clung to Greg's arm, looking up into his face. She had to make sure he understood why she had cooperated. She couldn't bear to see the hurt in his eyes. "Greg, about earlier... I just... there was a gun pointed at you..."

Greg placed one of his hands on top of hers, his eyes locked on hers. "I don't know what will happen next here at the Vault, but at least they recovered the drive before it could do any real damage. You don't have to worry about me. I know why you did it."

"Well, that's the thing," Adrianna stammered, trying to find the right words. "I didn't cooperate with them fully. My file was entirely on that drive because Jeremy was looking over my shoulder as he showed me what to do. He mentioned he was short on time, so I hoped he would only take a quick look at the rest of the files. For everyone else, I started the download of their information so it would look like I complied, but then I paused it immediately afterward, trying to corrupt and minimize the spread of those people's personal information. I know it was a risk, but I need you to know that I did my best to keep you safe, but I never intended to join those guys."

Instead of answering, Greg leaned down and gave her a big kiss on the lips. "That will definitely make things easier for whatever is to come."

A moment later, one man in a black SWAT uniform came over to them. "We need to question both of you. Sir, I need you to stay here until your escort arrives. Ma'am, please come with me."

With a glance at Greg, she followed him. That parting kiss reassured that maybe everything wasn't lost. A glimmer of hope grew in her chest as the man walked Adrianna out of the Vault. She tried to keep it at bay. She did not know how things were going to work out after today. This long day was only beginning.

They led Adrianna into a room with a table and chairs and a single overhead light that cast stark shadows on the walls. Her heart raced as she took her seat, feeling vulnerable and alone in the cold, sterile environment. She had always been a law-abiding citizen, and the thought of being interrogated by the authorities was beyond her wildest nightmares.

A stern-looking woman with her hair pulled back in a tight bun entered the room and sat across from Adrianna. "I'm Special Agent Moore from the FBI," she said, her tone devoid of warmth. "To get the full picture of what happened at the Limestone Vault today, I'll need to question you and ask you a few questions. I expect you to answer fully and truthfully."

Adrianna swallowed hard and nodded, her palms sweaty. The questions began, and Adrianna recounted the day's events, starting with her arrival at the Vault, the subsequent takeover by Jeremy and his accomplices, and her desperate attempt to protect Greg and minimize the damage caused by the theft of sensitive information. She emphasized her lack of allegiance to Jeremy and Joshua, and her efforts to resist their coercion.

They dissected and analyzed Adrianna's story for hours, sometimes veering into territory that felt invasive and personal, especially when it came to Greg. Her emotions swung from fear to anger and back again, but she clung to the knowledge that she had done her best to protect the man she was falling for and her colleagues in a dangerous situation.

As the hours ticked by, Adrianna grew increasingly exhausted, her eyes heavy and body aching. Finally, the interrogations ended, and Special Agent Moore led her to a small waiting area. Looking past the half a dozen other individuals in the room, she spotted Greg sitting on a sofa, drinking a coffee. He stood up immediately upon seeing her, almost spilling the coffee as he quickly set it on an end table. She walked over to him, her eyes never leaving his. With a vast sigh of relief, she collapsed into his arms.

"I missed you," Adrianna whispered, her voice breaking.

"I missed you too," Greg replied, his embrace tightening.

They stood there, holding each other in the sterile environment, as they waited for the verdict. *Would they be deemed innocent? Would the Bureau implicate them in the crimes committed by Jeremy and Joshua?* Eventually, Adrianna let go of Greg and slumped into the chair near his cooling coffee.

Greg walked over to a coffee pot, poured a fresh cup, and handed it to Adrianna before sitting beside her. "I'm so sorry you got caught up in all of this," he said, his voice low. "I should have been able to protect you better."

Adrianna shook her head, her eyes softening as she looked at him. "Don't be silly, Greg. You did everything you could to keep me safe, and I appreciate it more than you know. I never would have made it through today without you."

Greg gave her a small smile, but his eyes were still heavy with worry. "I just can't believe this happened on my watch. I'm supposed to keep this place secure, and I let someone slip through the cracks."

Adrianna reached over and took his hand, giving it a gentle squeeze. "You can't blame yourself for what happened. Jeremy and Joshua were determined to get what they came for, and they were willing to do whatever it took to get it. You did everything you could to stop them."

Greg leaned his head back against the wall, a heavy sigh escaping his lips. "I should have been more vigilant. There is just too much going on in my life right now," he said, his voice barely above a whisper, as if talking to himself.

Before Adrianna could ask him about his last statement, Agent Moore entered the room, followed by another agent that nodded at Greg. The two agents exchanged glances, and Moore cleared her throat before speaking. "After a cursory review of today's events, we have concluded that neither of you were complicit in the criminal activities perpetrated by Jeremy and Joshua. We believe you acted under duress and did everything in your power to minimize the damage caused by their actions. That being said, your clearances are being revoked until we can complete a more thorough investigation."

Chapter Thirty-Eight: The Case of the Clearances

A *drianna*

Adrianna heard a car pulling up to her cottage, and a moment later, a loud knock on the door. She peered out the window, and to her surprise, it was Greg. Her stomach felt like it wanted to tie itself in knots, and she plastered as much of a smile as she could muster on her face before opening the door. She wasn't leaving her cottage much lately, but was trying to keep busy honing her gardening skills, painting, and churning through a mountain of romance novels in her to-be-read pile. Unfortunately, nothing seemed enough anymore without Greg.

She had barely talked to him for days. The waiting to hear about the verdict on their clearances was painful, and Adrianna didn't know if she should keep working on memorizing investigation codes or start packing boxes. Things were just beginning to get interesting with Greg, but now whenever she and Greg got together, things instead seemed strained and stalled. It was as if neither one of them wanted to voice the bleak potential future looming in front of them. It was hard to move forward when they were stuck waiting to see how their current situation would play out. Here in the country, Adrianna didn't have many job options as a background processor who was not allowed to review people's backgrounds.

As she opened the door, she took an involuntary step back. The huge grin on his face did not match her more somber mood. "Do you want to come in?" she asked hesitantly, standing in front of her dead spider plant. She didn't want to have to explain to Greg how her plant, ironically named Greg, had died. A few days at home worrying about her future and the plant had gotten mushy in addition to its already poor brown color. An Internet search later, she realized that in her efforts to keep it alive, she had watered it too much.

Greg stepped through the door and wrapped her in a warm embrace. She snuggled in, enjoying the moment of comfort, not sure how many more they would share. After a moment, he pulled back to talk to her without letting go. "I just got the call that I can start work on Monday. Not only that, but they reinstated your clearance too!" he exclaimed. "Your manager will be in touch soon and will let you know when you can start back at work. They said it impressed them that you could act under pressure and protect people's personal information, even under duress. Since they recovered the flash drive with all your personal information on it, they feel Joshua lost his blackmail and his ability to unwillingly turn you into a sleeper agent."

Adrianna's face broke into a genuine smile. She could live the life she wanted again; her life was back on track. Now she could go back to reading about the crazy things happening in other people's lives, and hers could return to normal. She would get the chance to see where the new relationship with Greg would take them and give her feelings a chance to grow without the pressure of feeling like she might leave at any moment. Things would go back to the way they were. Normal, but with maybe a bit more spice.

Leaning up to Greg, she kissed him straight on the lips. Greg's eyes widened, but he leaned in and kissed her back with such fervor that the recent stresses melted away. Their lips moved in harmony as the heat between them built. She teased his bottom lip with her tongue, and she could feel his heart beating wildly against her chest. Greg leaned in, his demand for her pushing her back a few steps until she leaned against her kitchen counter. He pulled her closer to him, giving Adrianna the heady sensation of their bodies melting together.

Crash!

Greg's roving arm accidentally knocked the dead spider plant off the counter and onto the floor. Greg jerked backward at the crash, his eyes growing large. "I'm so sorry! I didn't mean to knock over your plant. If I repot it, maybe it will survive."

Adrianna laughed. "I don't care about the plant." She didn't need Greg the spider plant anymore because she had the real thing. Her perfectly handsome man, his single kiss, made her want nothing more in her life.

Regretfully, Greg pulled back and let her go as he bent down to pick up the pieces of the broken pot. Adrianna grabbed her broom and dustpan. After they mostly cleaned it up, Greg looked up. "Would you like to go see a local fireworks show with me tonight? The township is doing an end-of-summer show."

Adrianna nodded, excitement for tonight and their future bubbling within her. "Absolutely."

As they walked hand in hand to the car, Adrianna couldn't help but feel a renewed sense of hope for the future. She had her job back, her relationship with Greg was stronger than ever, and together, they had overcome what seemed impossible. The fireworks that they were about to watch seemed like the perfect metaphor for the bright, beautiful, and explosive love that was blossoming between them.

As they settled down on a grassy hill to watch the fireworks display, Greg wrapped an arm around Adrianna, pulling her close. The first explosion of color lit up the night sky, casting a warm glow on their faces.

Adrianna glanced at Greg, marveling at how lucky she was to have him in her life. "You know, sometimes life takes unexpected turns, but I wouldn't change a thing about what we've been through together."

Greg smiled, giving her hand a gentle squeeze. "Neither would I. We've proven that we can face anything as long as we're together."

The fireworks continued to burst in brilliant colors above them, each explosion illuminating the night sky and reflecting in their eyes. As the vibrant spectacle unfolded, they sat there, wrapped in each other's arms, feeling a deep sense of gratitude for the love they shared.

"It's beautiful," Adrianna whispered, her eyes fixated on the dazzling display.

"It is," Greg agreed, his eyes never leaving her. "But not as beautiful as you."

Adrianna felt her cheeks flush at his heartfelt compliment, and she leaned in to give him a tender kiss. As their lips met, another firework exploded overhead, casting a shower of colorful sparks around them.

As the fireworks display came to a breathtaking finale, Adrianna and Greg sat there, still wrapped in each other's embrace. The sky was filled with the last remnants of the colorful explosions, but their hearts were bursting with love and hope for the future.

As the night sky faded back to darkness and the sound of the fireworks echoed in the distance, Adrianna and Greg shared one last lingering kiss before gathering their things and heading back to the car. Hand in hand, they walked through the night, their hearts filled with love and excitement for the next chapter of their lives together.

For Adrianna, the future had never looked so bright.

Chapter Thirty-Nine: Epilogue

Adrianna

Greg pulled up to the Limestone Vault with Adrianna in the passenger seat. They carpooled to work together whenever their shifts aligned, and Adrianna was secretly enjoying the extra time spent with him. As he put the car into park, she turned to Greg with a smile.

"Ready for another day at work?" she asked cheerfully.

Greg returned her smile. "As ready as I'll ever be. It's always an adventure working at the Limestone Vault, but hopefully things will be calmer now that the whole fiasco with Jeremy is over, although it wouldn't surprise me if we have to revamp all of our security protocols in case Joshua tries to come back. I heard the security team is still trying to determine if he actually did anything or took anything the last time he was here. Whatever happened, he covered his tracks well."

Adrianna took a moment to process this last bit of information, then leaned over and gave him a quick kiss on the cheek. "Whatever your day looks like, I know you can handle it. Have a great day at work, Greg."

He grinned, rubbing the spot where she had kissed him. "You too, Adrianna. See you later."

With that, they both exited the car and made their way toward the entrance of the cave that housed the Limestone Vault. As they approached, they spotted two familiar faces, Dana and Charles, standing near the entrance waiting in line to get checked in. Despite the security buzzing around them, they only stared at one another, talking and laughing softly at each other, oblivious to everything around them.

Adrianna got in line behind them and gave them a warm smile. "I see you guys had your security clearances granted. Congratulations."

Greg extended his hand. "Welcome to the Limestone Vault! If you have any questions, don't hesitate to ask. Everyone here is pretty friendly."

"Thank you," Dana replied, still glancing at Charles. "We really appreciate the warm welcome." She finally looked away when it was her turn to go through security.

Adrianna scanned her badge and put her bags through the X-ray machine, while Greg walked off to join the other security guards. She walked down the tunnel to her room with Dana and Greg, but felt like the third wheel of a bicycle. When they arrived at their room, she nodded to them and politely said, "Well, I have to get to my workspace. Have a great day, you two."

As Adrianna walked away, she couldn't help but notice the chemistry between Dana and Charles. They seemed to be completely smitten with each other. She pegged them as perfect for each other so long ago, and it turned out she was right. She may not have done much to actually get them together, but maybe she had some matchmaker skills after all.

She walked by Judy's desk and tried to give a little wave, but the woman pointedly ignored her. *Well, I guess I can't win them all.*

As Adrianna approached her workspace, she spotted her friend and coworker, Henrietta, organizing her own desk. Her belly looked so big and hung low enough that it looked like the baby would fall out at any moment. "Hey, Henrietta," Adrianna called out. "Did you see the two new employees?"

Henrietta looked up from her desk, her eyes wide with excitement. "Yes, I did! Dana and Charles, right? They seem like a cute couple."

Adrianna laughed. "That's what I thought too. They couldn't take their eyes off each other."

Henrietta leaned in, whispering conspiratorially, "I heard they met right before they started down here and have been inseparable since orientation. Speaking of which, how are things between Greg and you?"

Turning red, Adrianna was too embarrassed to answer.

Henrietta winked at her. "That look on your face says it all! Now, let's get to work before our boss catches us gossiping."

Adrianna sat down at her desk and was soon happily typing away at her computer as she went through the day's work. It was nice to get back to work and feel useful. She had a giant stack of backgrounds to work through, but after the incident with Joshua, she would make sure that nothing slipped through the cracks. She'd witnessed the consequences of bribery or blackmail firsthand.

She worked through a case where a person had so many late credit payments and bankruptcies that her fingers got tired typing up her report. Another person admitted to illegal relations on business trips, and another spent two years of his life never leaving his bedroom. He played video games, and his mother brought food straight to his door.

Adrianna hoped the young man at least had a bathroom attached to his bedroom, but it didn't specify in the case.

One thing is for sure, this job is never boring. She sighed contentedly. Happy in her quiet little cubicle, she was looking forward to meeting Greg for a walk during her lunch break. This job gave her the perfect amount of quiet time she needed, while Greg and her friend Henrietta made sure she didn't become a complete hermit. It felt like she had finally found a good balance in her life. Adrianna pulled her attention back to her case files.

One particular case caught her attention: a man named Bob Kingston. On the surface, he seemed like a normal, upstanding citizen, with a prestigious educational background and an impressive employment history. However, as she dug deeper into his records, she found something strange. Each time she tried to verify his education and employment history, no one recognized his name. It was as if he didn't e xist.

Perplexed, Adrianna stared at the case file, wondering how someone thought they could pass a background check by lying about their entire history. That was when she noticed something else: the type of font on some letters in the file was slightly different. It was subtle, but noticeable if you looked closely.

A chill ran down Adrianna's spine and her brow furrowed as she questioned herself. "Am I being paranoid? Or is there something more to this?"

* * *

Would you like to read more? Join Cozy Adventure Club: https://reamstories.com/mirandaherald

Did you enjoy this story?

I would really appreciate your help by leaving a short, honest review in your favorite store. This not only helps me to gain visibility of my stories, but helps other readers find a good book that they would enjoy. Thank you in advance and happy reading!

What happens in Adventure Club stays in Adventure Club

I have an amazing opportunity for my readers- Join Cozy Adventure Club!

Members can receive:

Early access: Read my current work in progress earlier than on serial platforms and have access to the full book before it officially launches.

Library access: Read ALL of my previous books for one low price!

Cozy book club: Discuss your cozy reads and all the good feels with the author and other like-minded community members.

Exclusive bonus content: Get interviews with characters, deleted scenes, games, and more.

Sneak Peeks: Be one of the few with behind the scenes information. See cover art as its being created and learn the next book I'm writing before anyone else.

Come for the cozy adventures and stay for the memorable quirky characters.

Join my membership community for pre-release books and ex-clusive content!

https://reamstories.com/mirandaherald

10 Prequel Scenes from the Loves Cats Series
Excerpt from Willa's Blooper Reel

Katrina sorted all the fresh flowers into piles around her living room. *This smells wonderful. I hope they keep this powerful scent for the shower tomorrow.* She sat down in the only open space left on the floor and looked around her.

She had twenty-three flower centerpieces to finish by tomorrow. They were going to meet at eight in the morning to set up the hall for her sister, Susan's bridal shower. *I wish I had an easier time at work today. I was hoping to be fresher before tackling this.*

I'm just swamped at work right now. We had a lot of new cats come in recently. Last week, one of my volunteers told me they got a new job, and she doesn't have the time to help anymore. Another told me today that they were moving. It looks like I will be recruiting new volunteers next week.

Katrina picked up one of the glass vases and groaned. *This is going to take me all night, but what choice do I have? I guess I will have to stay up as late as it takes to finish this project.* She turned on the television in the background and filled the bottom of the vases with glass beads.

Willa sat napping behind her on the couch while she fiddled around with the flowers. Katrina tried a few different arrangements until she got the perfect look. She fiddled around with tying a perfect bow from the coordinating ribbon and then snapped a picture to send to her sister.

Good. One arrangement done, twenty-two to go. At my current rate of one flower arrangement per every half hour, that's only eleven more hours to go. Katrina put her head in her hands. *What have I gotten myself into?*

Katrina got to work. At one point, Willa came over and sat on top of a pile of flowers. "No, no, Willa. Come on. You can't sit there. You'll smash them. Here, it's almost dinnertime. Why don't I get you some food?" Katrina got up and poured cat food into Willa's dish. Willa munched happily as Katrina went back to work.

Luckily, now that she got the design down, she pumped out eight more arrangements over the next two hours. Katrina was midway through the next one when she decided that she really needed a break. She stood up, stretched her legs, and made some tea.

When she got back into the living room, she sat back down in front of her partially finished arrangement. *I thought I already put a purple one in there.* She picked up a new purple one. *I guess I didn't. The flowers are already running together.*

Katrina had twelve arrangements complete when she noticed that there were half as many of the yellow flowers as the pink and purple ones. *Oh no. The florist must have miscounted. I don't have enough yellow. What can I do? Maybe if we use the ones with yellow flowers on every other table, it won't be a big deal that some have yellow and some don't.*

She tried out arranging a centerpiece with no yellow flowers and added extra baby's breath so that they still looked full and put it beside the completed arrangements that had yellow. *I like it. Instead of being overwhelmed with yellow, it gives more of a hint of yellow.* Convinced it solved the problem, Katrina continued on.

Around two in the morning, Katrina was down to her last two arrangements. She was growing cross-eyed and developed a weird aversion to pink, purple, and yellow flowers. She reached for a flower to her side, when she realized that there were none of the pink flowers left.

Katrina became suspicious and looked around. *It's one thing if the florist miscounted the yellow flowers, but I recounted the pink and purple ones only a few hours ago. The only one other living thing in the house was… Willa.*

Katrina turned around to see Willa innocently sitting on the couch behind her. Unfortunately, the thief made a mistake. Upon closer inspection, she saw a yellow flower petal in her fur. Exhausted, she sternly asked, "Willa, what have you been doing with my flowers?"

Willa continued to look on, completely innocent. Katrina pretended like she was back at work, making another flower arrangement, while carefully watching the remaining purple flowers.

Out of the corner of her eye, she watched Willa silently pad over to the flower pile. She picked a flower up in her jaws and traveled behind the couch to sneak it out of the room, unseen. Katrina stood up slowly to see where she was taking the flower.

Willa turned the corner into her bedroom and climbed under the bed. There she laid her latest acquisition on-top of a nest of flowers she made. Immediately, she rolled all over them, crumpling the new flower to match the other ruined flowers.

Katrina felt like she could cry. *I worked so hard on these arrangements all night. I'm so close to finishing. Where am I going to get more fresh flowers at this time of night?* She gently scolded Willa for taking things that weren't hers. Willa lowered her head and slunk further under the bed, knowing she was caught.

Katrina picked up the scattered pieces of flowers. *There's no salvaging these. I simply don't have time to go pick up new flowers tomorrow morning. These last two centerpieces were for the head table. I can't just set them up there with a few purple flowers and some leftover baby's breath flowers.*

Willa looked out under the bed and softly meowed. A cranky Katrina scowled. "Maybe I should put you in one of the centerpieces. At least then it would look full. Then Susan could bring her cat, Biscuit, to put in the second one. It would look perfectly full and balanced." The offhanded comment sparked an idea in Katrina's mind.

The next morning, Susan gushed over the flower arrangements. "I can't believe you finished these all yourself! They turned out beautiful and smell great too."

A bit about Miranda Herald

Typing by moonlight and powered by tea, I love reading and writing whenever I can fit it in. I find a good mind boggling puzzle or escape room exhilarating and was excited to include them in my latest works. I hope you enjoy my puzzling twist on romance and join my characters for many more adventures!

I love to hear from my readers and want you to join my community on Facebook, Tiktok, and Instagram. Check out my website to find all of my freebies, novels, and social links. You can find everything at my website **www.mirandaherald.com.**

Join my membership community for pre-release books and exclusive exclusive content!

https://reamstories.com/page/mirandaherald